"Thank you for putting up with me this afternoon," said Coco.

The expression in her blue eyes made Benjamin's chest knot. "It wasn't anything. I just want you to feel better," he said, and squeezed her shoulder.

She rose on tiptoe and surprised the heck out of him when she brushed her soft lips across his jaw. "It was a big something to me," she countered, then left.

Benjamin rubbed his jaw where she'd kissed him. He wondered if the rest of her was as soft as her lips. He wondered what her lips would feel like on his body. He wondered what kind of sounds she would make if he kissed her and touched her all over.

Crazy, he told himself. If there was one woman he shouldn't even be thinking about taking to his bed, it was Coco. She was too important to him because of his daughter Emma.

Coco was off-limits and he was damned determined to make sure he didn't forget it.

Dear Reader,

Have you ever wondered if you were switched at birth? What if you were actually an heiress to millions? Or what if you were actually royalty? I mean, really, doesn't the title Princess sound a lot more fun than Miss or Ms.?

Well, our nanny heroine, Coco Jordan, is an ordinary girl and she wasn't switched at birth. She was adopted, and her parents have passed away. She has no family, and she's focused on helping rancher Benjamin Garner bond with his motherless infant daughter. Coco's life is turned upside down when she finds out her birth father was a prince, and Benjamin steps in to help protect her from all the unwanted attention from the press. But can Benjamin's protectiveness turn into love? Stay tuned.

And about that first question of wondering if I was switched at birth…I actually feel as if I hit the jackpot with my parents because of how much they have always loved and encouraged me. If you get a chance to read Coco's story, I would love to hear from you at leannebbb@aol.com.

Wishing you love and laughter,

Leanne Banks

A HOME FOR NOBODY'S PRINCESS

LEANNE BANKS

Recycling programs
for this product may
not exist in your area.

ISBN-13: 978-0-373-65698-1

A HOME FOR NOBODY'S PRINCESS

This edition published by arrangement with Harlequin Books S.A.

For questions and comments about the quality of this book please contact us at CustomerService@Harlequin.com.

www.Harlequin.com

Printed in U.S.A.

Books by Leanne Banks

Harlequin Special Edition

The Prince's Texas Bride #2115
The Doctor Takes a Princess #2127
§*A Maverick for Christmas* #2151
††*The Princess and the Outlaw* #2198
††A Home for Nobody's Princess #2216

Silhouette Special Edition

Royal Holiday Baby #2075

*The Royal Dumonts
†The Billionaires Club
**The Medici Men
§Montana Mavericks:
The Texans Are Coming!
††Royal Babies

Silhouette Desire

**His Majesty, M.D.* #1435
The Playboy & Plain Jane #1483
**Princess in His Bed* #1515
Between Duty and Desire #1599
Shocking the Senator #1621
Billionaire's Proposition #1699
†*Bedded by the Billionaire* #1863
†*Billionaire's Marriage Bargain* #1886
Blackmailed Into a Fake Engagement #1916
**Billionaire Extraordinaire* #1939
From Playboy to Papa! #1987
***The Playboy's Proposition* #1995
***Secrets of the Playboy's Bride* #200[illegible]
CEO's Expectant Secretary #2018

Other titles by Leanne Banks available in ebook format.

LEANNE BANKS

is a *New York Times* and *USA TODAY* bestselling author who is surprised every time she realizes how many books she has written. Leanne loves chocolate, the beach and new adventures. To name a few, Leanne has ridden on an elephant, stood on an ostrich egg (no, it didn't break), gone parasailing and indoor skydiving. Leanne loves writing romance because she believes in the power and magic of love. She lives in Virginia with her family and a four-and-a-half-pound Pomeranian named Bijou. Visit her website, www.leannebanks.com.

This book is dedicated to the babes:
Coco, Ann, Terri, Mina, Rose, Peggy, Sharon, Jane,
Kathy, Kathy, Kim, Sandy, Catherine, Terry.
You are a constant source of inspiration to me.

Chapter One

His daughter hated him.

Benjamin Garner carefully opened the front door to his sprawling two-story house and paused. Even though he was six foot four and had been described as two hundred pounds of muscle due to the hard work he put in on his cattle ranch of over ten thousand acres, he'd become a stranger in his own home.

Why? Because his five-month-old daughter couldn't stand him.

Every time he came toward her, she gave a shriek that would wake the entire country of New Zealand, and New Zealand was a good fifteen-hour flight away from the town of Silver City, Texas.

He stepped as lightly as he could in his boots. Coco

Jordan, the young nanny who had seemed to work magic with baby Emma from the first time the two had met, had assured him that Emma could sleep through regular environmental noises, but he didn't quite believe her.

Sometimes Benjamin wondered if his daughter had special powers and could smell him or hear him breathe even from the front door when she was upstairs in the nursery. Benjamin scowled at himself. This just showed what a nutcase he was becoming.

His dog, Boomer, limped out to greet him. Boomer had been one of his best herding dogs, but after he'd gotten his leg twisted in some barbed wire, he couldn't run fast enough. Benjamin figured the dog had earned his retirement, so Boomer spent his days trying to catch scraps from his housekeeper's cooking and dozing on the sofa. Benjamin reached down to give the mixed-breed dog a rub on his head, but was quiet about it. At least his dog liked him.

Heading for his office at the back of the house, he strode past the kitchen.

"Ah!"

His stomach knotted. He knew that sound. He knew that voice. He kept on moving.

"Benjamin." The low, sweet voice of the nanny called to him. "You can't avoid her forever."

"Ah!" Emma said.

Taking a deep breath, he turned and faced the two of them, standing in the kitchen doorway. His daughter stared at him with big blue suspicious eyes, while

Coco was all soft, pretty encouragement. Emma wasn't screaming—yet. Maybe she was just gearing up for it.

"She just finished eating, so she should be in a good mood. Don't you want to hold her?"

Hell, no, he thought. A rattlesnake was easier to handle. He shifted his hat back and shrugged. "I haven't washed up."

"That's okay. A little dirt won't kill her."

"Okay," he said, opening his arms, preparing himself for his daughter's rejection of him. "I'll hold her."

Coco moved closer and Benjamin noticed that Emma's eyes seemed to grow larger with each step she took. "Here you go," she murmured to Emma. "This is your big strong daddy and he will always take care of you. There's no need to be afraid of him. He's on your side."

Coco gently placed Emma in his arms and he drew her close to his chest, holding his breath. Emma stared up at him, her eyes wide. He counted silently. One. Two. Three. Four. Five.

She pressed her lips together and glanced toward Coco. As soon as her lower lip jutted out in a perfectly defined pout, he knew what was coming. His daughter let out a high-pitched sound of distress that quickly grew in volume. He met Coco's discouraged gaze and shook his head.

"Here," he said, handing Emma back to the nanny. "There's no need to torture the poor thing. That's why I hired you."

Coco patted Emma on the back in a soothing motion. "But we have to get her used to you. We have to find a way—"

"Maybe by the time she hits her first birthday, she'll like me better," he said and turned away, tamping down his own sense of discouragement.

"Wait," Coco said, and he felt her hand on his arm.

He glanced over his shoulder.

"Maybe she doesn't like your hat," she said. "Maybe if you take it off, she'll—"

"I'll give it a try next time," he said. "Right now, I need to enter some stock updates on the computer. Later," he said and strode the rest of the way to his office.

His muscles twitched. He could manage this ranch with one hand tied behind his back, but he couldn't hold his daughter for even one minute without scaring her so much she shrieked in fear. Somehow, someday, he needed to change that, but he didn't know how to do it.

He scrubbed his forehead with his hand. What had Brooke done? He wondered if his ex-lover had told Emma he was a horrid man. He wondered if, before Brooke had died riding on the back of her most recent lover's motorcycle, she had corrupted Emma's brain. Was that even possible?

He and Brooke had shared a sexual affair that had lasted a weekend. He'd come to his senses, as had she. Until weeks later, when Brooke had learned she was pregnant. Benjamin had immediately proposed, even though he and Brooke had both known they didn't belong together. She'd refused his proposal but accepted his support. He'd reluctantly realized that he would be a twice-a-month father. He only saw Emma three times before her mother's death.

Suddenly he'd become a full-time single father. Who made his daughter cry at the very sight of him.

His gut clenched again. Sometimes he wondered if he would ever hold her without her screaming in fear.

Sucking in a mind-clearing breath, he focused on the computer screen. He wasn't going to fix his problem with Emma today. Thank goodness he had Coco. Emma felt safe with her. That was why he had hired Coco. She was magic for Emma. She had been the first time she'd held her. Somehow, Coco was an ordinary woman with superpowers when it came to babies, which was exactly what Benjamin needed. Lately, he'd wondered if she could be…more…

Benjamin shook his head. Crazy thoughts. His computer cursor was blinking at him. He should enter the appropriate numbers in his Excel spreadsheet.

There was plenty of trouble in his day before he even thought of Coco.

Coco stared after her tall, broad-shouldered boss as he disappeared into his office. She jiggled Emma to help her settle down. The baby clung to her like a tick, bless her heart. Coco was certain Emma still missed her mama even though her mama had been the type to come and go as she pleased.

Coco was pretty certain Benjamin had tried to hire Emma's previous nanny, but not everyone wanted to live on a ranch in the middle of nowhere, Texas. Nowhere, Texas, suited Coco just fine after all the days she'd spent with her mother in hospice care. It was nice not to have to live by herself in a tiny apartment, always aware that she wasn't just alone for the night. Now that her mother had passed away, Coco was truly alone in this world.

Caring for a baby was therapeutic for Coco. Even though Emma was terribly insecure and frightened, she represented light and hope to Coco. After the strange visit Coco had received yesterday from the even stranger two men who had shown up on the front porch of Benjamin's home, though she'd shooed them away, she was afraid. What did they want from her? Was there some other debt her mother had owed that Coco would need to pay?

She panicked at that prospect. By the time her mother had passed, there'd been nearly nothing left. Coco had taken out a loan so that her mother could have a proper burial and she would be paying college loans for a long time. Coco had quit just shy of getting her degree and was determined to finish it. But that was for later. Now, she just needed to get some of her equilibrium back. From the first moment she'd stepped onto this ranch, something had clicked and she'd known this was the place for her. It didn't hurt that Emma needed her.

Benjamin's long-time housekeeper, Sarah Stevens, made a clucking sound as she entered the hallway. "How long is it going to take that man to just sweat it out and hold that baby until she stops crying?"

"I can't totally blame him," Coco said. "Emma hasn't been at all cooperative."

Sarah's generously lined face softened. "Well, it's true the baby has been through a lot of changes. Who knows what kind of environment she was living in with that Brooke Hastings." Sarah gave a snort. "Party girl. Don't know how he ever got involved with her."

Coco had kept her curiosity to herself about the odd pairing of one of Dallas's most notorious party girls and solid rancher Benjamin Garner. "They must have seen something in each other."

Sarah snorted again. "Enough for a fling. Of course, as soon as Benjamin found out little Miss Brooke was pregnant, he tried to do the right thing and offered to marry her, but the woman refused. She didn't want to be tied down. Too much life to be lived."

"Did she keep partying throughout her pregnancy? That could have been terrible for Emma."

"I think Brooke dialed it down during the pregnancy, but as soon as Emma was delivered, she was hitting the circuit again. Thank goodness you showed up when you did. The little peanut was usually okay with me as long as I held her every minute, but I couldn't get anything done around the house. I'm still catching up," she grumbled.

"It was good timing for me, too," Coco said. "But I may need to take a couple hours off soon for personal business."

Sarah sighed. "It's only fair. You've been working two weeks straight with her. I just know that I'll be the fill-in." The older woman lifted her finger to Emma's cheek and cracked a smile. "She's adorable when she's not screaming."

"I'll try to schedule my break when she's taking a nap," Coco said.

"You're overdue," Sarah said. "We'll just have to adjust. Maybe I'll finagle a way to get Benjamin together with her. Never would have believed a little baby could scare the devil out of a man like him," she said and laughed. "You let me know when you need your break. I'll be here for the little one."

"Thank you, Sarah," Coco said and wondered if perhaps she should just take Emma with her. She was reluctant to cause any more trauma for Emma or Benjamin.

Later that night, Coco slept in the room next to the nursery. The baby could still be a bit unpredictable. Coco was still bothered by the men who had come to visit her and wondered what she should do. Were they bill collectors? Should she consult a lawyer? It took her hours to go to sleep

A shriek jerked her awake. Coco sat upright, adrenaline pumping through her as she tried to pull herself together.

Another shriek pierced the air and she realized it was Emma. Another bad dream, she thought. Who would have guessed that a baby could have bad dreams? Coco jumped out of bed and darted out of her room toward the nursery next door. She didn't bother with a light because she knew the way by heart.

Except this time she plowed into a human wall.

She felt her breath leave her body in a rush. Automatically bracing herself, she put her hands on his shoulders. Hot flesh over sinewy muscles. Her heart slammed against her ribs. She felt his arms slide around her to stabilize her.

Coco's eyes finally began to adjust to the darkness. "Sorry," she managed, a strange sensual panic racing through her.

"I heard Emma and she wasn't stopping," Benjamin said in a rough voice that made goose bumps rise on her arms.

Coco took a step back. "Sorry," she said again. "I was fast asleep."

"You need a break," he said, raking his hand through his hair.

"We'll figure it out," she said and pushed through Emma's partially opened door. The volume of Emma's screams increased exponentially without a pause. Coco rushed to the crib and picked up the baby, cooing at her.

"There you are," she said. "You're fine. You're okay, sweetie. You don't need to be upset. You're safe."

Emma alternately whined and made hiccupping sounds.

Coco hated that the baby was so upset. She bobbed up and down. "There you go. See. You're okay."

Emma gave a heavy sigh. Then another. She felt the tot fasten her mouth against her shoulder and make buzzing noises and couldn't help laughing under her breath.

"I take it she's okay," Benjamin said from a few feet behind her.

Emma continued her happy buzzing noise and Coco turned around to face Benjamin. He was dressed in a pair of pajama pants and nothing else. "Sure sounds like it to me."

Emma paused a half beat then continued.

"Why does she keep waking up screaming?" he asked, resting his hands on his hips, clearly perplexed.

Jiggling Emma, she stroked the baby's back. "It's not every night. She's just still adjusting. I think she'll calm down soon."

"She has an appointment with the pediatrician soon. Maybe he can tell us something. I'll want you to go to that appointment," he said. "If I take her, she'll just scream the whole time."

"That's fine. I'd like a few hours off tomorrow or the next day, though. I have some personal business to take care of."

"No problem. Sarah will cover for you. I may need

to hire someone part-time so you'll have backup," he said with a sigh.

"We can give her a little more time. With little ones, they can turn a corner before you know it." Coco could feel Emma's rigid frame start to relax against her. "Maybe she wouldn't be so afraid of you in the dark. Come closer and see."

"I did that earlier," he said in a dry tone.

"But this is different. It's dark and you're not wearing your hat. Maybe—"

"Maybe not tonight," he said firmly. "I don't want to get her riled up again tonight. See you tomorrow," he said and left the room.

Coco slid into the rocking chair with a sigh. She hated that Emma and Benjamin were so tense around each other. When she'd first accepted the position to take care of Emma, she'd thought Emma's screaming when her daddy came close was just a phase. True, it had only been a few weeks, but it seemed as if the two of them were growing more tense with each other, instead of less. Benjamin wanted to avoid upsetting Emma, which gave them fewer opportunities to interact.

Coco wondered if she should just set Emma in his arms and leave so the two of them could work it out, but she knew that was probably her lack of sleep talking. She felt Emma's sweet little body go limp with relaxation. The baby's trust in her never failed to grab her heart. Rising, she returned Emma to her crib and went back to bed. This time, she fell asleep before her head hit the pillow.

Late the next morning, after Coco put Emma down for her morning nap, she dressed to go into town. Just as she descended the steps from the front porch, she saw a black Mercedes pulling toward the front of the house. Her stomach dipped. This was the same car that had brought the strange men who'd visited her two days ago.

Sweating, she glanced over her shoulder, praying that no one would see the visitors. Her heart pounding in her chest, she walked toward the vehicle as it stopped.

The man in the passenger seat opened the door and rose from the car. He was short with gray hair and squinty eyes. "Miss Jordan, my name is Paul Forno. I represent the House of Devereaux. My associate and I need to discuss an important matter with you."

The *House of Devereaux?* Coco wasn't sure if it was a fashion label or a collection agency. When the driver opened his car door, panic raced through her. "Listen, this is private property. This is also where I work."

"Yes, ma'am. Please accept our apologies, but this is news that must be delivered in person. If you could give us a few moments of your time—"

"Not right now," she said. "I'm on my way out."

The man sighed. "As you wish, miss, but we don't have a lot of time. Please accept my business card and call me at your earliest convenience," he said and offered her the card.

Confused, but not wanting to show it, she gave a brisk

nod, stuffed the card into her small purse and strode to her car. *We don't have a lot of time.* What could that possibly mean? And who was *we?* Her hands shook as she stuck the key into the ignition of her five-year-old economy car. Looking in her rearview mirror, she felt a microbit of relief when she saw the black Mercedes pull away from the ranch.

Coco opened her car window and took several breaths. The men looked like the same kind who had frequented her mother's home the last two months before she died. Her mother had fallen deeply in debt, and lenders had become impatient with her inability to pay her bills. Coco had helped as much as she could, but near the end she was only working part-time. Her mother's care had required the rest of her time and energy.

She wondered if somehow she was responsible for some of her mother's bills. She'd never cosigned loans, but she had used a credit card when they'd had an electrical problem and her car had needed an emergency repair. She'd thought she'd paid it off, but now she thought she needed to review her check register.

Her mind reeling, Coco drove off the property onto the highway into town. All the time, she wondered what she should do. She remembered a friend who had been a legal assistant. Maybe she could call her.

Reaching the small town of Silver City, she pulled alongside the town diner and got out of her car. She wanted a good cup of coffee or hot chocolate or hot apple cider and maybe a little sympathy from her friend Kim, a waitress at the diner. She'd known Kim back in high school, and Kim had since married and moved to Silver City. Coco and Kim had shared a meal when Coco had first come to town last month. Since then, Coco had dropped into the diner with Emma a couple times.

Coco walked inside the homey diner and the hostess immediately greeted her. "How are you doing, miss? Can I seat you?"

"Fine, thank you. Yes," Coco said. "Please do. Just one."

"We've got plenty of room. I'll put you in a booth."

As soon as Coco slid into the red booth, Kim Washburn winked and waved at her. Coco shot her a weak smile in return.

A couple moments later, Kim trotted to Coco's table. "Where's the little one today?" Kim asked.

"I finally got a couple hours off so I left her sleeping with Sarah at the ready to take over. I need to run some errands."

"I would say so. You haven't taken a break since you signed on for this gig, have you? What can I get you?"

"Hot chocolate," she said. "Or apple cider."

Kim laughed. "You want both?"

"No. I'll take hot chocolate with extra marshmallows."

Kim studied her thoughtfully. "Something wrong? Now that I think about it, you don't look too happy."

"Just distracted," Coco said.

Kim shrugged her shoulders, but clearly didn't believe her. "If you say so. But if you need some help, I'll give it my best try," she said, then headed for the kitchen area.

Coco bit her lip. She was so used to fending for herself that she almost didn't know how to accept help when it was offered. Kim returned with a mug of hot chocolate overflowing with marshmallows.

Coco smiled. "Thanks. Can you keep something confidential?" she asked in a low voice.

"Sure, what is it?"

"I may need some legal advice," Coco said reluctantly.

Kim's eyes widened and she slid into the booth across from Coco. "Well, you're not married, so you don't need a divorce. I can't believe you've committed any crimes."

"It's not that," Coco said. "I just need to check on what happens to a person's debts when they die. I need to know if I'm responsible for my mother's debts."

"Well, I can tell you that. As long as you didn't co-sign anything, you're not responsible. How do I know? When my husband Hank's parents died, they had a boatload of debt and none of the kids had to pay. Now the repo company took everything his parents owned and that meant no inheritance for the kids, but the kids did not have to pay." She frowned. "Why are you worried?"

"These strange men have come to Benjamin Garner's house. They remind me of the bill collectors who kept coming around when my mother was sick," Coco said.

"Well, if they're angling to get some money out of

you, they're just crooked. You should tell Benjamin. He'll take care of them in no time."

"But he's my employer. It would be embarrassing to have to tell him about this," she said.

"If they keep coming around the house, he's going to find out anyway. Better to nip it in the bud. And trust me, there's no one better-suited to take care of someone trying to pull some sort of money scheme on you than Benjamin." Kim thumped the table with her knuckles. "I gotta get back to work. Enjoy those marshmallows and talk to Benjamin."

Coco stared at the marshmallows, her stomach churning at the prospect of discussing her mother's debt issues with Benjamin.

"She's okay as long as I bob up and down. I just hope it doesn't make my fillings fall out. You'll have a high dental bill if that happens," Sarah warned Benjamin as she jiggled Emma.

Emma had spotted him and was throwing a hard glance at him. It amazed him that a kid under six months old could kill a man with her eyes. Maybe she was a chip off the old block after all. He turned to go to his office.

"Not so fast," Sarah called. "The least you can do is come here and say hello to your daughter."

"I'll just make her cry," he said.

"I'll take that risk. You can't run from your own child forever," she said.

"I'm not running," he said. "I just don't see any need in upsetting her."

Benjamin slowly walked toward Sarah and Emma. The baby glared at him like a gunfighter ready for action.

"Boo," he said in a low voice.

Both Sarah and Emma gasped. "Why'd you do that? You're just gonna scare her even more."

Benjamin shrugged and walked closer. He lifted his hand to the sweet skin of the baby's chubby arm. "Hey, Princess, sooner or later, you'll realize that I'm gonna be around a long time. I can just tell you're gonna give me hell till you figure that out."

Emma frowned, but she didn't cry. She shot him another hard look and stared at his hat.

"Does this bother you?" he asked, removing the hat from his head and extending the Stetson toward her. He thought about the sweet nanny he'd hired. At first sight of the woman, Benjamin had sensed a tender heart. "Coco said it might."

Emma stared at the hat then at him and for one sliver of a second, he saw a softening in those intense blue eyes of his daughter.

The front door opened and Coco's footsteps sounded in the foyer. He knew her step already. Benjamin automatically turned and Boomer limped to greet her. "Hey, boy," he heard her say to the dog. Seconds later, she appeared, breathless, clearly a little concerned. "How was she?"

"Ah!" Emma said.

"She's fine as long as I jump up and down," Sarah said in a grumpy voice as Emma stretched her hands toward Coco. "Did you take care of your business?"

Coco's gaze darkened, taking Emma into her arms. "Mostly, but I—uh—I'd appreciate it if I could maybe talk to you sometime soon," she said to Benjamin.

Surprised, he shrugged. "No problem. Just let me know when. I'm in the office this afternoon and I have a cattlemen's meeting tonight."

Coco stared at him for a moment. "So when is a good time?"

He got an odd feeling in his gut at the expression on her face. He hoped this didn't mean trouble. Benjamin didn't need one more iota of trouble in his life. And he sure as hell didn't need trouble from his daughter's nanny. He'd hired the woman to alleviate his problems, not exacerbate them.

"I can see you up until six today or after nine tonight," he told her.

She took a deep breath. "After nine. Emma will be in bed by then."

He nodded and placed his hat back on his head. "Nine o'clock. Come to my office."

"Can we, uh, meet in the den?" she asked, surprising him with the request.

He shrugged. "Okay. See you at nine. I've got work to do," he said and walked away.

That night, just before 9:00 p.m., Emma fell asleep with no struggle. Coco set the baby on her back in her crib. Emma was totally relaxed and Coco had a feeling the baby might sleep through the whole night. She quietly walked from the room and left the door open just a sliver. She had a monitor, but Coco liked the idea of having more than one modality to hear Emma if she cried.

Now she was second-guessing her decision to talk with Benjamin. She'd almost hoped Emma would take a long time to get to sleep, so she wouldn't be able to meet with him. Her stomach knotted with nerves. Benjamin was a tough man. She just hoped he would be on her side.

Chapter Two

Coco hesitated at the entry to the den. Now she wondered why she'd chosen it with its brown leather furniture and masculine tan, rust and brown palette. Maybe the office would have been better.

Suddenly, Benjamin stood in front of her. Her heart stopped.

"You look like you need a drink," he said.

She shook her head. "No. I'm fine."

"Hmm," he said doubtfully. "Come on in."

She followed him into the den and gingerly sat across from him on the sofa. He'd sat in the well-worn leather chair. He looked at her expectantly and her throat went dry.

She opened her mouth and a croaking sound came out.

He set his shot glass next to her on the couch. "You need a swallow of something. May as well be some good whiskey."

She took a sip of the alcohol. It burned all the way down.

"Another," he said.

She hesitated, but his nod encouraged her and she took a second sip. "Enough," she said and gave the glass back to him. "I need your help."

He took a swallow from the squat glass he'd shared with her. "I figured that. What's the problem?"

"I'm not sure. These men have been trying to see me."

"Men?" he repeated, a shot of displeasure rising through him.

"They've already come to the house twice and—"

"Which house?" he asked, sitting up in his chair.

"This house," she said. "Your house."

"Why in hell are they coming here?" he asked. "And why haven't any of my staff seen them?"

"They're here to see me." She pulled a card from her purse and handed it to them. "I have no idea who the House of Devereaux is." She took a quick, desperate breath and pushed her brown hair nervously behind her ear. "As you know, my mother died a few months ago. She didn't have much money at the end." Coco bit her lip. "Bill collectors started coming around. These men reminded me of them."

Benjamin frowned and set down his drink. He studied the card. "Did you cosign any of her loans?"

She shook her head.

"I'll call my brother—he's an attorney—and see if he knows anything about this House of Devereaux. In the meantime, if those guys show up, I want you to call my cell right away."

She looked hesitant.

"Is there anything else I need to know?" he asked.

She shook her head. "No. I'm just not sure I should have dragged you into this."

"These men came onto my property without an invitation. You are an important employee. That makes it my business."

The vulnerability she showed grabbed at him, although he sure as hell wouldn't admit it. Coco had a fresh-scrubbed face and slim body, making her look younger than her years. Sweet and innocent, probably hoping for a Prince Charming to sweep her off her feet. Not his type at all. Benjamin had usually gone for low-maintenance women who knew their way around a man and wouldn't expect too much of him. Except for Brooke. He'd made a big mistake with Brooke.

"I need your word that you'll call me if they come around again," he insisted.

She sighed and nodded reluctantly. "I will, but I'm hoping I'll fall off their radar."

Benjamin had a feeling that her wish wouldn't come true. "Just so we understand each other," he said and stood. "I'll see you tomorrow."

* * *

The next day as Coco dressed Emma, she pointed to the photograph of Benjamin she had placed on a dresser in the baby's room. "Daddy," Coco said. "That's your daddy."

The baby was cheerful and a little less clingy than usual. Coco was pleased with Emma's progress and hoped there might be an opportunity for Emma and Benjamin to make a little peace.

The doorbell rang as she was feeding Coco her lunch.

Sarah entered the kitchen. "Two men are here to see you. Dever-something?" she said.

Coco's stomach clenched. She wondered if she should send them away, but remembered her promise to Benjamin. She swallowed over the lump in her throat. "Tell them to wait in the front room, please," she said and pulled out her cell phone. As soon as Sarah left, she punched Benjamin's number on her cell phone.

"Benjamin," he said in a curt voice.

"It's me, Coco," she said. "The men are here. They're in the den."

"Do you know what they want?" he asked.

"Not yet. I've been feeding Emma. I only called because you made me promise," she said.

"I'll be there as soon as I can," he said and hung up the phone.

Coco handed the feeding of Emma over to Sarah and made her way to the front room. The two men immediately stood. "Miss Jordan, thank you for seeing us.

Again, I'm Paul Forno, and this is my colleague Gerald Shaw."

Tense, Coco laced her fingers together in front of her. "If this is regarding my mother's debt, I'm afraid I can't help you."

Mr. Forno's face crinkled in confusion. "Your mother's debt?" he echoed. "I wasn't aware that Miss London had any debt issues. According to our information, she's been well cared for, per her agreement with your father."

"Miss London," she echoed, not certain who was more confused—she or Mr. Forno. "That's not my mother's name. You must have the wrong person."

Mr. Forno studied her. "You do know that you were adopted, don't you?"

"Of course, but—" She broke off, struggling to keep her emotions under control as she tried to make sense of the men's visit. "Is this about my birth mother? I tried to find her years ago, but I was told she didn't want to meet me. Has she changed her mind?"

Mr. Forno exchanged a look with his associate. "Unfortunately—"

The front door opened and Benjamin stepped inside, his gaze sweeping the front room. "Problem?"

Coco immediately felt a sense of relief. "I think there's a lot of confusion right now."

Benjamin addressed the two men. "It shouldn't take long to clear up any confusion given the fact that you've been bothering Miss Jordan. If you have a legitimate reason to see her, then spill it or leave."

Mr. Forno cleared his throat. "This is a matter of a delicate nature. We, uh, prefer to speak to Miss Jordan privately."

"That's up to Miss Jordan," Benjamin said.

"I'd like Mr. Garner to remain," she said. "Whatever you say to me, you can say in front of him."

Mr. Shaw sighed. "Then, sir, we must request that you sign a confidentiality agreement."

"I'm not signing anything," Benjamin said. "You're in my house and you're wasting my employee's time and mine, too."

Mr. Shaw looked nervous and perplexed. "Then I must beg of you to keep what we are about to tell you in the strictest confidence."

Benjamin lifted one shoulder in halfhearted agreement. "Still waiting."

Mr. Forno waved his hand. "Allow me to introduce ourselves, Mr. Garner. I am Paul Forno and this is my associate, Gerald Shaw, with the House of Devereaux. Perhaps we should sit down."

Impatience simmering from Benjamin, he sat down. The others followed.

"As I said, we are representatives of the House of Devereaux," the man began.

"What is that?" Benjamin asked.

Mr. Shaw blinked. "The royal House of Devereaux. The ruling family of the country of Chantaine."

"Never heard of it," Benjamin said.

Mr. Forno looked at Coco and she shrugged. "Sorry. Neither have I."

"Oh, my," Mr. Forno said. "Chantaine is a small, but beautiful island country off the coast of Italy. The Devereau family has ruled the country for centuries."

"And what does this have to do with Coco?"

Mr. Forno sighed. "Your birth mother was Ava London. She had a long-term relationship with Prince Edward of Chantaine and you are—" He cleared his throat. "A product of that relationship."

Coco frowned, blinking at the man's announcement. Her birth mother? Her birth father? After all these years, she would learn who they were? She shook her head in amazement. "Are you saying that Ava London and Prince Edward are my biological parents?"

"Yes, they are," he said.

She was so stunned she couldn't comprehend it all. "My father is a prince?"

"Yes, he was," Mr. Forno said.

"Was?" she echoed, her heart racing. "Oh, my goodness! Is he alive? Is my birth mother alive?"

"Unfortunately, no. His Royal Highness passed away several years ago, and his son, Stefan, has since ascended the throne. Your birth mother passed away just over a week ago," he said.

"Oh," she said, feeling a surge of sadness. Since her mother had died, she had felt so terribly alone. She'd had no close relatives, no siblings.

"What does this mean for Miss Jordan?" Benjamin asked.

"Well, the House of Devereaux wishes to extend an invitation for you to visit the country of Chantaine and also to meet the Devereau family," he said brightly.

"Visit Chantaine? But how?" Coco asked.

"The usual way these days," Mr. Forno said, continuing to smile. "A transatlantic flight."

Her mind whirling, she looked at Benjamin and she immediately knew she couldn't go. He was counting on her. Emma was counting on her. She shook her head. "Oh, I couldn't. I've just started working here and Emma needs me. Thank you for the invitation, though," she said.

The men looked surprised. "You're turning down the invitation to meet the Devereaux."

"It's not a good time for me or my employer," she said, glancing at Benjamin, who was wearing an expression of shock.

"Are you sure about this?" he asked.

"Of course I'm sure. I've made a commitment. I have every intention of keeping it," she said and stood. All three men were gaping at her as if she'd grown an extra head. Her mind was racing. She finally knew who her biological parents were. She also knew they hadn't wanted her. She had a brother, a prince, who probably wasn't thrilled with her existence. "Are there other Devereaux? Do I—" She stopped at the insane thought. They weren't her full brothers and sisters, yet she couldn't tamp down her curiosity. "Did Prince Edward have other children?"

"Yes, he did," Mr. Shaw said. "There's Prince Stefan, Princesses Valentina, Fredericka, Bridget, Phillipa and Prince Jacques."

Mr. Forno and Mr. Shaw exchanged a look. "Prince Edward also fathered another child with your birth mother. A son."

"Another," she said, disbelief racing through her. "My, he was quite the busy one, wasn't he?"

Mr. Shaw cleared his throat, but didn't respond.

Benjamin gave a low laugh. "I have to agree."

His chuckle distracted her from her own state of shock for just a few seconds. "Now, let me get this right. You're telling me that my birth father has six—no, wait, seven—other children. And one of these is my full biological brother. I have a real brother? Where is he?" she wanted to know. "Who is he?"

"He's currently in Australia. An engineer. He's been quite difficult to reach," Mr. Shaw said. "We aren't at liberty to give any more information about him. However, the news could break at any moment."

"News?" Benjamin repeated. "I thought you said this was a confidential matter."

"It is, but we fear the news of Prince Edward's newly discovered children could be leaked to the press any day," Mr. Shaw said.

"That's why you've been so determined to get to

Coco," Benjamin said. "Why you've invited her to Chantaine. Control Coco and you can control the spin."

"It's quite understandable that the Devereaux would like to have an opportunity to meet with Miss Jordan," Mr. Shaw said in a snippy voice.

"Hmm. Well, this is a lot for Miss Jordan to take in, so I'm sure you don't mind giving her some time to process it."

"Of course," Mr. Shaw said. "If she would just sign a release stating she won't discuss the matter with the press—"

"She's not signing anything without an attorney looking at it," Benjamin said.

"Sir, it's in her best interest not to discuss this publicly. Once the story breaks, she'll be flooded with requests from the paparazzi. Signing this document will provide her with an easy excuse to avoid interviews."

"She won't need an excuse," Benjamin said and rose to his feet. "Now, as long as she has your contact information, I think we're done for the day."

Both men appeared disappointed. "Call us if you change your mind about the release or visiting Chantaine," Mr. Forno said to Coco.

Her mind was reeling with all the information, and Benjamin was right. It was going to take some time for her to digest it. "I don't think I'll be changing my mind, but I have your phone number," she said and watched as the two men walked out the front door.

She felt Benjamin's gaze on her. "You okay?"

Not wanting to appear as rattled as she felt, she lifted her chin. "Of course I'm okay. The news is a bit bizarre, but I've always known I was adopted. I also knew that neither of my birth parents wanted to meet me. Now I know why."

Sarah walked into the room. "Are they gone? Good. I was in the middle of placing my grocery order. Do you mind taking the baby?" she asked.

"Of course not," Coco said, automatically holding out her hands for Emma.

Sarah quickly walked away and Coco caught a whiff of why the housekeeper was eager to have Coco take Emma. "Someone needs a change," she said and tapped Emma on her nose. "Excuse me. Duty calls."

"Just a minute," Benjamin said.

"Trust me. Waiting will just make this worse," she said and headed down the hallway toward the stairs. She heard his footsteps behind her as she made her way to the nursery.

Feeling Benjamin's presence behind her, she quickly changed the messy diaper and picked up the baby. Coco turned to face him. "Thank you for being with me during the announcement."

"I'm not sure you realize what an impact this could have on you," he said. "Your father was a prince. It's possible you have an inheritance. Hell, in a way, you're a princess," he said, with a hint of horror in his eyes.

Coco scoffed and jiggled Emma as she fussed at the sight of Benjamin. "Oh, that's ridiculous. I'm no princess, that's for sure. I'm sure there's no inheritance for me. They would have mentioned that right off the bat," she said and took in his doubtful expression. "Wouldn't they? After all, I'm illegitimate. They've probably got all that sort of thing covered. I can't believe Edward was the first man in the Devereau family to spread his seed. I mean, some men just can't keep it zipped and—"

She stopped when she realized Benjamin might construe her words as criticism of him. "I mean, he fathered, or *sired,* eight children. That's different than one or two or—"

"It's okay. Let me know when you want to get in touch with the Devereaux," he said.

"When?" she said. "That will never happen. They don't really want me. Their father never wanted me, either." She suddenly felt vulnerable because she'd been so sure before that she was alone in the world. She'd coached herself to believe that she would be okay. Now she could hardly believe what she'd just been told—at the same time, she sensed that her newfound family wouldn't welcome her. "I have enough going on in my life. I don't need to—"

"You'll change your mind," he said.

She scowled at him. "You can't know that."

He hooked his thumbs in his pockets. "I know you will. At some point, at some time, you're going to want to meet those brothers and sisters. Anyone would want to know their relatives, especially if they thought they had none. I would," he said.

"Would you?" she asked.

"Yeah," he said. "I've got three brothers. Two in town and one up in Claytor Junction, Colorado. They've always been important to me. More so after my dad died and my mom took off for Costa Rica."

"Costa Rica?" she echoed.

Benjamin shrugged. "Mom always wanted to travel. Except for a few vacations, she just waited until after my dad died to do most of it. It's her way, she's running. One day, she'll stop."

Coco gnawed the inside of her lip. "You don't resent her? Don't you wish she was here?"

Benjamin laughed. "Hell, no. She needed to go. My dad's death was hard on her. I'm glad she had the guts to get out of town. Everyone has to mourn their loss in their own way."

"Is that why you got involved with Brooke?"

He paused a long time then sighed. "Maybe. I had to be strong for a while there. None of my brothers wanted to take over the ranch and it was going to be a big job."

"Why didn't they want to help?" she asked.

"They don't have ranching blood in them. One is a lawyer in town. One is an investment specialist. The other's a computer specialist. That left me," he said.

"I don't know much about ranching, but it looks like you're doing a pretty good job."

He cracked a half grin. "Thanks. I am doing a pretty good job."

Emma made an unhappy sound. "And if I can get

my daughter to stop crying every time she sees me, I'll be in good shape."

"You can start by taking off that hat," she said.

"I don't know if that makes a difference," he said.

"Give it a try," she said.

Sighing, he removed his hat.

Emma stared at him in silence.

"I can't believe it's the damn hat," he said.

The baby extended her hand out to his face.

"Lean closer," Coco said.

He slid her a doubtful glance, but bowed his head toward the baby. Emma gave a disapproving growl. Yet, the baby extended her hand to Benjamin's chin.

"Ah!" Emma said.

"Improvement," Coco said, unable to withhold a trace of victory in her voice.

Enduring the baby's probing strokes across his mouth and chin, he grimaced. "That's a matter of opinion."

"She's not screaming," Coco said.

"True," he said, gumming at Emma's tiny finger.

The baby's eyes widened and she pulled back her hand.

"Don't scare her," Coco scolded.

"How ya' doin', darlin'?" he asked Emma.

Her rapt gaze held his and she waved her hand at his face. "Ah!"

"Ah!" he echoed and caught her hand within his. "You're my girl. Don't ever forget that," he said and kissed her hand. "Ever," he said.

Emma kicked her feet and stared into his eyes, but for the first time in forever, she didn't scream. Maybe Coco was right. Maybe the hat had frightened her. More important, maybe Coco was right and he needed to chill and just love his child. That assignment could be a bit more difficult than he planned.

Over the next few days, Coco tried to ignore the new information she'd received about her birth family. Her birth parents had never wanted her. Her half brothers and sisters weren't truly interested in her. If so, wouldn't one of them have come to meet her? And what about her full brother? He apparently couldn't give a flying fig about her existence.

The knowledge stung, but after her father had died, a part of Coco had always been fearful. One day, her mother would die. She knew that one day she would be all alone in the world. For a while she'd believed that was a long way off, but then her mother had gotten cancer and everything had gone downhill.

Staying with her mom during her last days had been the most important, yet the hardest thing she'd ever done. Coco had hoped it would give her peace, but since her mother had passed, she'd felt restless. She'd wake up in the middle of the night in a panic.

Taking the job with Benjamin and Emma had given her a strange sort of relief. Emma had immediately responded to her as if there were already a bond between the two of them. Even though Emma was jittery, there was a sense of calm to the daily routine. Although Emma screamed and cried, she also smiled and cuddled. Something about the baby soothed Coco's sadness. She wanted to help heal Emma's fear. In the short time she'd spent at the Garner ranch, she'd grown extremely protective of Emma and was determined to bring peace between the baby and her daddy.

At this point in her life, nothing else was more important.

Each hour, however, she felt herself grow a little more curious about the royal family. In her few spare moments, she checked out the Devereau family and Chantaine online. Most of the siblings looked snooty to her—except for the one with curly hair named Phillipa. Coco was surprised to discover that one of the princesses—Valentina—actually lived in Texas with her husband and daughter.

Her half sister was in the same state. She could actually drive to meet her, she thought. That said, Princess Valentina might have no interest in meeting her. In spite of the fact that she insisted she had no expectations of her new semisiblings, Coco felt restless day and night. When she went to bed, her mind whirled with possibilities. In the deepest, darkest part of her, Coco wanted family—sisters, a mother, a father, cousins, aunts, uncles. Her adoptive mother and father were dead. Her birth mother and father were dead. She'd thought she was all alone. Was she? Was she crazy to think she *wasn't* alone?

* * *

The next day, Coco strapped Emma to her chest and took a fishing pole and tackle box out to one of the streams on the Garner ranch. In Texas, people took their infants out to do things that celebrated everything great about the state. That meant the general population wouldn't be surprised to see an infant at a professional ball game, fishing or even horseback riding, with their mama or daddy, of course. Thinking back to all the fishing trips she'd taken with her daddy before she'd turned ten, she cast her line into the stream, sat on the shore and waited. And waited. And waited. Then she got a bite and reeled in a medium-sized trout. She threw him back and cast her line again.

Early on, she'd learned that waiting was a big part of the game. Her father had made that easier with stories he'd told her—stories he'd clearly conjured. She reconstructed one of those stories and repeated it to Emma, who promptly fell asleep.

Hey, it was a cool story even if it made Emma snooze. Coco caught another three fish that she tossed back into the stream. One of Benjamin's workers stopped by to chat with her for a few minutes, and by late afternoon, she felt great. All her worries had disappeared. She gave Emma a bottle. The sun was shining on her head, she was sweating just a little bit and she began tramping back to the house.

Back at the house, Benjamin paced his office. Coco and Emma were gone. Coco had told Sarah she was going fishing, but Benjamin hadn't gotten around to showing her the real fishing spots on the ranch. So how the hell had she gone fishing?

He thought about Tweedledee and Tweedledum, the two guys representing the Devereau clan who'd visited Coco. He wondered if, despite their dweebiness, they had darker motives. What if they had gone after Coco and his daughter?

Benjamin headed for the front door, intent on tracking down Coco and Emma when he saw Coco stomping up the steps with a fishing pole, a tackle kit and a beaming smile.

Her smile was contagious. "You look happy."

"I am," she said. "I caught four fish and threw them back in the stream."

"You could be lying," he couldn't resist teasing. "What proof do you have?"

Her eyes darkened. "Your daughter is a witness."

Benjamin looked at his sleeping daughter and laughed. "She's a bad witness."

"You don't believe I caught those fish?" she asked, lifting her chin.

"Why should I?"

"Because I told you and because I'm an honorable woman. The only tales I tell are the kind that keep you occupied when you're waiting to score a fish. My daddy told me a lot of those kinds of stories when we went fishing," she said.

He met her gaze and felt a strange sensation in his

chest. She'd surprised him. He wouldn't have expected her to be a fisherman even though he'd known she'd grown up in a small town.

"And you're trying to teach my daughter how to fish at five months?" he said, nodding toward the baby pack on Coco's chest.

"Do you mind?" she asked.

"No. I don't mind. It's good for her to get outside."

"Do you want to take her?" she challenged.

Whoa, he thought. "She'd scream bloody murder if I tried to take her fishing."

Her eyes softened just a little. "I'm not talking about fishing. I'm talking about you and your daughter doing something enjoyable together. Both of you need that."

Chapter Three

The next night, Benjamin met his brother Jackson at a bar in town. They sat down over couple of cold beers. "So, what's up?" Jackson asked. "You don't look too good."

Benjamin slid a sideways glance at his younger brother. Jackson, an up-and-coming lawyer, had always been fast on the draw. He'd finished high school in two years, college in three, then gone on to collect his law degree at a prestigious university.

"Wanna trade places for a month or two?" Benjamin joked.

"Sorry." Jackson lifted his mug to his lips. "Even I know you would get the easier deal. Ranch and a new baby. Me? I'm a single guy with no plans for a wife or kids anytime in the next century."

"I hadn't planned on children yet, either," Benjamin said wryly but couldn't keep from cracking a smile. "How's the practice going?"

"Good," he said. "It would be easier if I were in Dallas, and there was that offer in New York."

"So why don't you go?" Benjamin challenged, already knowing the answer. His brother was committed to Silver City.

Jackson shrugged. "I don't know. This just feels right."

"Then quit bellyachin' about it," Benjamin said.

Jackson shot him a mock-hard glance. "You're the one who wanted to trade places," he said and took a swallow of his beer. "What's going on?"

Benjamin sighed. "Besides the fact that my daughter hates my guts?" he asked.

Jackson appeared to swallow a laugh and took another sip of beer to cover it. "That could be tough."

"Yeah," Benjamin said.

"But there's something else," Jackson prodded.

Benjamin sighed again. "The new nanny."

Jackson frowned. "I thought she was magical. She calmed your screaming daughter. She was perfect."

"Close to perfect," Benjamin muttered. "But we've hit a bump."

"She's illegal?" Jackson asked.

Benjamin shook his head. "No. It's worse that that."

"What could be worse?"

Benjamin looked from side to side and leaned toward his brother with a low voice. "She's a princess."

"What?" Jackson asked loudly.

"Keep it down," Benjamin said with a scowl.

"What are you talking about?" Jackson whispered.

"She was given up for adoption and she just found out her father was a prince."

"Holy crap," Jackson said. "You know how to pick them."

Benjamin frowned. "Thank you for your support."

"What do you need from me?"

"Some representatives of the royal family tried to get her to sign some forms," Benjamin said.

"Absolutely not," Jackson said. "Let me take a look at them first."

"I already said no. They've invited her to visit their island country, but again, they want her to sign papers. She says she doesn't care about meeting them, but I think she does."

Jackson scrubbed his face. "And you're wondering what this means legally? Do you want to fire her?"

"Hell, no. Emma loves her," Benjamin said.

"Okay. Well, there's a remote possibility that she's due an inheritance, but since she's out-of-wedlock and an adult, it's unlikely. Royals have ways of tying up their funds."

"I'm sure Coco would appreciate the infusion to her

bank account, but there are other concerns," Benjamin said.

"Such as?" Jackson asked.

"Such as the royal reps said she would be contacted by the media when the news breaks," Benjamin said.

Jackson winced. "That's true. There's a huge infatuation with anything royal. She could get pestered…."

"My men and I can handle a little pestering," he said.

"This might be more than a little," Jackson warned.

"I think she wants family," Benjamin said. "She didn't have any brothers or sisters growing up. Her father died when she was young and her mother died within the last few months."

Benjamin felt his brother studying him.

"This is starting to sound personal. Do you have something going on with your baby's nanny?"

"No," Benjamin said immediately. "I'm just telling you what I've observed."

"So, no hanky-panky. No kisses. No middle of the night sleepwalking into each other's beds."

"No."

"Hmm," Jackson said, drumming his fingers on the bar as he studied Benjamin. "I don't know. What does she look like?"

His brother's intent expression irritated Benjamin. "There's nothing going on between Coco and me. Between Brooke and the baby, trust me, I've had enough trouble with women lately. Emma feels safe with Coco. The last thing I want to do is mess up that situation."

"Well, if you have any more legal questions or if I can give you a hand with anything, let me know. Since you're more likely to saw off a leg than ask for help, you must consider this more important."

"Yeah," Benjamin said and decided to change the subject. "Who's in your fantasy football lineup?"

He and his brother talked football for a while, then Benjamin headed home. He noticed the porch light and floodlights were on and wondered if Sarah had left them lit. After a blazing-hot summer, Benjamin welcomed the cooler temperatures. He could almost see a hint of vapor when he exhaled.

Pulling open the front door, he stepped inside and cut the lights.

"Wait!"

He immediately identified Coco's breathless voice and turned the lights back on. "What are you doing?" he asked as he saw her trotting toward the steps.

"I just needed some fresh air, so I walked around the house a few times. I've got a remote intercom in case Emma wakes up," she said, pushing her hands into the pockets of her hoodie sweatshirt as she walked up the steps. Her nose was pink and her cheeks were flushed from the cold.

"How long have you been out there?" he asked.

"Not that long," she said. "I'm okay. I just didn't want to get locked out."

He sensed a restlessness vibrating from her. She

pushed back the hood of her sweatshirt and pulled her hair free. "You sure there's nothing wrong?" he asked.

"No," she said, but she didn't meet his gaze. "I used to walk around my mom's house that last month she was alive. Sometimes I just feel better after walking a little bit."

"I can understand that. I get itchy if I stay still too long," he said.

She finally looked at him. "Really?"

"Yeah, really. You want a cup of something to warm you up? It smells like Sarah may have left something warming in a crock."

"Apple cider," Coco said. "And it's delicious."

They went to the kitchen, and Coco pulled down the mugs and poured the cider. Benjamin took a sip too soon and it burned his tongue. "Ouch," he muttered and waved a hand for her to join him at the small table in the kitchen nook.

Coco smiled and sat across from him. "It smells so good. It's hard to wait."

She looked so young and sweet she could have been a teenager.

She met his gaze. "You're looking at me strangely. What are you thinking?"

"I'm remembering how I had to look at your driver's license twice before I believed you were twenty-four," he said.

Coco laughed. "I've always looked young for my age. My mother always told me there would come a time that I would appreciate that quality. Hated it in high school, though."

Benjamin took another sip; this one didn't scald his tongue, thankfully. "So, what made you want to do your little 5K around the house tonight? Have you been thinking about your new-to-you family?"

Coco's smile fell and she sighed. "I don't know what to do. I have a hard time believing they really want to meet me. It's not as if they've been beating down the door or calling me."

"There may some legal reasons that they're waiting for you to contact them," he suggested.

"Really?" she said, more than asked, in disbelief. "Well, all I know is if I had found out that I had a sister or brother, I would try to meet them."

"Then why aren't you?"

She shot him a dark look. "Because I don't like to go where I'm not wanted."

"You don't really know that you're not wanted," he said and leaned toward her. "Listen, if you want to go to Chantaine and meet them, we can work something out."

"I don't know how," she said, staring into her mug and cradling it with both hands. "Emma isn't settled in yet. She needs more time to feel at home and to get into a routine."

"That's true, but she'll get there," he said, even though he sometimes wondered if his daughter would ever feel at ease in his house. He was damn determined to do what was necessary to make it happen, though. "I don't want you to feel that you can't go," he said.

She bit her lip. "It's not like I would have anything in common with them."

He stared at her for a minute. She looked young, but he knew she'd carried a lot on her shoulders while her mother was sick. She'd taken charge with Emma and dealt with the baby's nightmares with no complaint.

"What are you scared of?"

She took immediate offense. "I'm not scared."

"Sure looks like it to me," he said.

"Well, I'm not. But you have to admit that these people are definitely in a different league."

He shrugged. "Still gotta put one sock on at a time."

She shot him a sideways glance and her lips twitched. "Unless they have a servant who puts on their socks for them."

Benjamin laughed. "That would be pretty pathetic." He put his hand over hers. "You don't have to make any rash decisions. You can take your time. Give yourself a break."

She met his gaze and took a deep breath. "I guess you're right. I don't need to work myself into a frenzy over this."

"Exactly," he said, and the moment stretched between them. The warmth in her eyes gave him a strange feeling in his gut. Realizing that his hand was still covering hers, he quickly pulled it away. It was one thing to try to comfort his daughter's nanny, but he didn't want Coco to misconstrue his sympathy as something else.

He cleared his throat. "Well, I should hit the sack," he said and rose to his feet.

"Me, too," she said, following him to her feet. "I'll take care of the mugs."

"Thanks," he said, wondering why his voice sounded so rough. He headed toward the doorway.

"And, Benjamin, thank you for talking me down from that cliff I was climbing," she said to his back.

He smiled at her description of her emotional state. "No need to scale a cliff unless it's absolutely necessary. G'night."

"G'night," she said as he entered the hallway. He felt another twitch at the sound of her soft voice, and he rubbed his stomach. He'd better take some antacid.

Two days later, as she was about to feed Emma, Coco saw Benjamin enter the house. Midlift of the spoon, Coco thought about the fact that Benjamin had been avoiding his daughter once again. She couldn't allow this to continue.

She pulled the spoon back from Emma. "Benjamin," Coco called as the baby frowned at her in confusion. Emma's soft, plump lips puckered in disapproval.

Benjamin poked his head in the doorway. "Yeah?"

Coco immediately stood. "Emma's ready to be fed and I…uh…I need to powder my nose."

Benjamin wrinkled his brow. "Powder your nose?"

"Use the ladies' room," she said.

Realization crossed his face. "Oh, okay. You want me to watch her?"

"I actually want you to feed her," she countered.

He frowned. "*Feed* her?"

"It's not that hard," she said and reached for his Stetson, but he was faster. "She hates your hat."

"I *like* my hat," he said.

"You don't need to wear it in the house while you're feeding a baby," she said and held out her hand for him to give her his hat.

"I'll put it on the table in the foyer," he said, lifting his hat from his head.

"Ah!" Emma called.

"Oops, better hurry. She's getting impatient," Coco said.

"Well, she can wait one minute," he said.

"Not unless you want her to start screaming so much she can't stop," she said. "Gotta go," she said, covering her ears as she ran to the upstairs bathroom. She wasn't sure she could hear Emma's screams at full blast and not respond.

She went into the bathroom closed the door behind her and turned on the fan. "La-la-la-la-la," she said as she covered her ears, determined to prevent herself from hearing Emma's screams. She continued for several moments then stopped her la-las. No baby shrieks pierced the sound of the fan. Giving in to her curiosity, she cut it off.

Still no sounds of alarm. Gingerly, she opened the bathroom door and listened. Silence greeted her. Coco felt a spurt of hope and tiptoed down the stairs.

"There ya go," Benjamin said. "Another bite. You're getting stronger. You're a Garner. You've got to be ready for everything."

Coco couldn't help smiling at Benjamin's words. When Emma gurgled, she had to cover her mouth to keep from giggling. She knew that sound signaled they were nearing the end of mealtime.

Peeking around the corner, she watched Emma give a huge raspberry, sending her latest bite of food and drool all over Benjamin's shirt.

"Whoa," he said and glanced down at his shirt. "What's up with that?"

Emma shot him another raspberry. This time, he had the sense to back away. "You got some power with that," he said, laughing as he wiped off his shirt with a napkin. "Do you do this every time you eat? It's a wonder Coco hasn't quit. I guess this means you're done."

He dabbed at her face with a napkin and she scowled and screeched at him. "Ah, you don't like the cleanup. Well, that's what happens when you're messy. You gotta get clean."

He wiped at her face and she screeched again.

Coco decided it was time to intervene. "I usually sing a song right now."

He glanced at her. "Nice of you to show up."

She bit her lip, but couldn't conceal a smile. "Well,

it looks like my timing is perfect. Seems that you two worked it out," she said.

"Temporarily," he said. "She sure can spit."

"I try to cut it off before that point. Once she starts gurgling, it's the beginning of the end."

"What's the magic song?" he asked.

"Wash your cheeks," she sang in a soft voice. "Wash your mouth. Shine like a sparkly star. That's what you are," she said and tapped Emma on her nose. "A sparkly star." Feeling sheepish, she shrugged. "I'm a triple threat with my deep lyrics, incredible vocal range and the ability to clean a baby's face at the same time."

"But can you dance and lasso cattle?"

"I don't know. If I tried to lasso cattle, then it might look like I was dancing," she said. "You want to pull her up from her high chair?"

He shot her a blank look. "Why would I want to do that?"

"Because she's finished eating and needs to get out of her chair, and the two of you need to get used to each other," she said.

Benjamin sighed and she noticed that his eye twitched slightly, but he unfastened Emma from the high chair and picked her up in his arms. The baby stared at him for a moment, then looked away and started making babbling noises.

Benjamin glanced at Coco. "What does that mean?"

"She's allowing you to carry her," Coco said and couldn't withhold a chuckle. Benjamin appeared as if he were carrying a live grenade and it would go off at any moment.

"What do I do now?"

"She's probably due for a diaper change," Coco said, goading him just a bit.

He shot her a dark glance. "I think the smashed pea shooting is enough for one day."

"In that case, carry her upstairs and I'll join you in a minute or two," she said.

"What am I supposed to do for that minute or two?" he demanded.

"Bond with her."

Benjamin groaned and walked into the hallway.

Coco cleaned up Emma's messy high chair and counted to three hundred. Carefully, she crept up the stairs to stand outside the nursery. She heard Benjamin talking. Peeking inside, she saw Benjamin pick up one of Emma's bunnies and move it from side to side in front of the baby.

Emma reached for the stuffed animal and squeezed it for a few seconds then dropped it.

"Oops," Benjamin said, reaching down to scoop up the bunny. Emma reached for the bunny again and dropped it again. "Fickle little thing, aren't you?" He caught sight of Coco and gave a nod.

"I see you've reached a peace agreement," she said.

"For now," he said and handed the baby to Emma.

"You just need to keep spending a little time with her. Soon enough you'll be giving her horseback-riding lessons," she said as she put Emma on the changing table and changed her diaper. "Helping her learn to ride a bike, then teaching her how to drive." She looked up to meet his horrified gaze.

"Driving," he echoed and shook his head. "Maybe she won't want to drive."

Coco laughed. "Now you're just dreaming."

"Let's take this one step at a time. The next step for me is to change out of this shirt that's covered with strained green peas." He glanced from Coco to Emma to Coco again. "See ya later," he said.

As soon as he left, Coco turned to Emma. "Good job!" she said. "You'll make a daddy out of Benjamin Garner before you know it."

The next day, Benjamin rode on horseback to check fences with one of his assistant foremen, Jace. Jace was young, but a hard worker, and both Benjamin and his foreman Hal valued good work ethics in their employees.

"Looks like there could be the beginning of a problem in the northeast corner," Jace said from his horse.

Benjamin lifted his binoculars and nodded. "Good catch."

"I should be able to get to it this afternoon," Jace said.

"That'll work," Benjamin said. "Let's check the other pasture, then we'll be done."

"Hal mentioned that we should be on the lookout for strangers coming on the property," Jace said.

"Have you seen anyone?"

"No. Hal also said it was something to do with the new nanny. She's not in danger, is she?"

"No," Benjamin said. "Coco's fine."

"Well, speaking of the nanny, she sure is nice," Jace said.

Benjamin glanced at Jace. "How would you know?"

"I met her when she was going fishing one day. Looked like she was pretty good at it," he said and laughed. "For a woman. I was wondering if it would be okay if I asked her out sometime."

"Coco?" Benjamin said.

"Yeah. She's pretty and nice. She seems like she would be fun."

"No," Benjamin said instinctively and without hesitation. He didn't have to think it through.

"No?" Jace echoed, clearly surprised.

"No," Benjamin repeated, bemused by the odd gnashing feeling inside him. "We're trying to get the baby used to living here. Coco is the most important ingredient in that equation. I don't want her distracted or bothered."

"I wouldn't bother her," Jace muttered.

"That's right. She's off-limits. Feel free to spread the word to the rest of the men," Benjamin said. With no female employees besides his housekeeper, Sarah, dating hadn't been an issue, until now. Even though Coco was attractive and appeared *fun,* he didn't want any additional complications in the picture with her. There were enough with the whole royalty thing. He hoped she would be able to put that on the back burner, but if she couldn't they would have to work something out. He had to think about what was best for Emma, and what was best for Emma was Coco.

Coco dressed Emma in a light jacket, tucked her into the stroller and took her for a walk. There was a slight nip in the air, but it was sunny and the time outside would do them both good. Coco headed for the back of the house, where a trail divided two fields. Chatting about the cattle and the trees, Coco alternately walked and ran. Emma let out a giggle when Coco ran.

"So you like a little speed in your stroller, do you?" Coco asked, glancing at the baby. "Your daddy's not gonna be happy if you feel the same way when you get your first car." Coco ran and Emma giggled again.

She turned around to return home, alternately walking and running. As she approached the back of the house, though, she noticed that Emma had fallen asleep, her head drooping to the side and her baby lips gently parted. Her heart twisted at the sight of her, so relaxed and at peace. As she rounded the corner to the front of the house, she wondered if she should take her up to her crib for a quick little snooze before dinner.

Three men and a woman immediately lunged toward her. She heard the click of cameras in between their questions.

"Miss Jordan, is it true that you are the illegitimate daughter of the former Prince of Chantaine?"

"Who are you?" Coco asked, shocked by their approach. She instinctively stepped in front of the stroller to protect Emma. "How did you find—"

"Your Highness," the woman began, "how does it feel to become a princess? You must be so excited."

Coco shook her head in confusion, distracted by the man shooting photographs of her. "I'm not a princess."

"Is it true that the Devereau family wishes to deny your place in the royal family?" a man asked.

Emma began to fuss.

"What place?" Coco asked and turned to pull Emma from the stroller. What a ridiculous question, she thought.

"Your rightful place in the royal family," the man said. "Surely you know you're due certain rights and privileges."

"Not really," Coco said as Emma began to wail.

"But you're a princess now," the female reporter said.

"I'm not a princess," Coco said flatly. "And you're making the baby cry. Are you proud of that?" she said more than asked and walked up the steps to the front door.

Chapter Four

"What I want to know is how in hell four reporters got past my men," Benjamin said to his foreman.

"We haven't been policing it 24/7, Ben," Hal Dunn said. The two had known each other since Benjamin was eight years old and Hal had been a young new worker on the ranch that Benjamin's father had then owned. Now Hal was Benjamin's right-hand man. "They could have sneaked through the wooded area in the front of the property."

"Well, I don't want to hear about anyone sneaking in anywhere," Benjamin said. "And 24/7 starts now."

"Got it," Hal said. "But I can tell you that whoever pulls that midnight shift is gonna want extra pay."

"Done," Benjamin said. "Just don't make it too much

or you'll get squabbling over who gets to take the night shift."

"That's for darn sure," Hal said with a rough laugh then turned sober. "Hope they didn't upset the little one or the nanny too much."

"Coco said Emma started crying but stopped as soon as they stepped inside the house. Coco seemed pissed off, but I think she may have been more rattled than she wanted to admit. I don't think she really expected any extra attention from the press, even though we were warned."

"Well, hell, she's royalty. That's big news around here," Hal said. "Maybe big news everywhere."

"Because it's going to change the world if Coco is a princess," Benjamin said with more than a touch of sarcasm.

Hal gave a combination of a wince and shrug. "Guess that's true. What else do you want us to do?"

"Just guard the perimeter," Benjamin said.

"Will do," Hal said.

A few moments later, Coco bounced down the stairs with Emma bundled in a fleece outfit "We're ready to go to the doctor," Coco said.

"What?" Benjamin said. "Why does she need to go to the doctor?"

"It's a regular appointment," she said. "Remember, you told me you wanted me to go with you?"

"Yeah, I remember," he said, thinking he should have added the appointment to his cell calendar schedule.

He must have put it on a different calendar. Having trespassers on his property had gotten him sidetracked. "Maybe I should have someone drive you to the pediatrician," he mused.

"Absolutely not. If we start behaving differently, then we'll have to do it for the next year. There's no need for such insanity."

"I could have one of the men follow her," Hal said.

"No," Coco said. "If we take the casual route, then the press will back off,"

Benjamin gave it a second, and even third, thought. "I think it would be a good idea to have one of our men backing you up."

"Overkill," she said.

"Better safe than sorry," he said, enduring her scowl. "We have to think about both your safety and Emma's safety."

Her complexion paled. "I would guard Emma with my life."

"I know you would," he said. "But I don't want it to get to that point."

She took a deep breath and nodded. "Okay."

Benjamin scrubbed his jaw with his hand. "I'll reschedule my other appointments for this afternoon. I need to stay on top of Emma's health."

Coco blinked and took a quick breath. "Uh, okay. That's a great idea. You just need to remember to take off your hat."

Benjamin felt Hal's confused gaze. "Emma doesn't like my hat."

"Damn," Hal said. "That's a shame."

"Tell me about it," Benjamin said and sighed. He took off his hat and clutched it in his right hand. "Let's go," he said to Coco and led the way to his SUV.

"Her car seat is in my car," she said.

"No problem," Benjamin said and transferred the seat from Coco's car to his. He watched as Coco wedged Emma into the car seat and shook his head. "Bet she hates that."

"If you give her enough toys, she forgets about it," she said. "But I'm glad we don't have to go on any long trips."

"You and me both," he said as soon as everyone was buckled in place.

He pulled away from the house and drove down the long drive to the public road. He noted a few cars parked alongside the public road and frowned but hoped they weren't newspeople.

Driving toward town, he checked his rearview mirror, relieved when it didn't appear that he was being followed. "So what's the purpose of this appointment? Any shots?"

"It's a regular checkup. Yes to the shots," she said.

"Damn," he muttered. "One more opportunity for her to associate me with pain."

"They really do forget quickly," she said.

"I'll let you hold her during the shots," he said.

Knowing the bond between Emma and Benjamin was still a bit tenuous, she acquiesced. “This time,” she said.

He slid her a sideways glance. “This time?”

“Yes,” she said. “There may be times when Emma will need support. She may break a leg—”

“Not on my watch,” he insisted.

She smiled. “She may fall and need stitches.”

“You'll teach her to be careful,” he said.

“Accidents happen. How many broken bones and stitches did you get when you were growing up?”

“That's different,” he said. “I'm male.”

“Ooh,” she said, drawing out the one syllable in a way that clearly indicated she disagreed. “Big mistake to think that because she's female, she won't have accidents. Plus there are illnesses that could take her to the hospital.”

Benjamin's stomach turned. “I don't like the sound of any of this.”

“Too late,” she said. “You're already her father. The good news is that you can take this all one step at a time. Plus you're already the type to man up, so you've got that on your side.”

Benjamin turned the corner to the road where the pediatrician's office was located. “What makes you so sure about that?”

“You wouldn't have gone after Emma right after Brooke died if you weren't a responsible man. You wouldn't have hired me ASAP. You wouldn't have taken off your hat for Emma and allowed her to spit peas at you."

"Well, I guess there's that," he said dryly and brought the car to a stop in front of the pediatrician's office.

"Do they give you a beer after this?" he asked.

She laughed. "No. Not until you get home. Let's go. It won't be as bad as you expect."

Automatically returning his hat to his head, he ushered Coco out of the car and freed Emma from her car seat. She was staring hard at him.

"Hat," Coco prompted.

"Oh. Okay," he said and removed it again, setting it in the front seat.

He handed off Emma to Coco and escorted them inside. They sat in the waiting room for fifteen minutes. Afterward, Emma was weighed and measured while they waited for Dr. Apple.

The jovial man walked into the examination room with a friendly, booming voice. "Hello to Emma and mom and dad."

"You didn't read the report. Emma's mother died last month. Coco is her nanny."

Dr. Apple frowned. "Oh, please accept my condolences. This must be a difficult time for you."

"Yes, but not in the way you're thinking," Benjamin said. "Emma's mother and I weren't married."

Dr. Apple's mouth formed a perfect O.

"Yeah, and Emma hates me. She screams bloody murder every time I come around," Benjamin said.

"She's not screaming now," Dr. Apple said.

"This is the exception," he said.

"Not true," Coco said. "All you have to do is take off your hat."

Benjamin couldn't deny her statement.

"Hmm," Dr. Apple said. "Let's check out your baby."

The doctor conducted the examination and ordered the vaccinations. Emma was above average in her weight and height. She had gained in both since her last appointment. According to Dr. Apple, Emma was thriving. Benjamin was certain the primary reason for that was Coco.

The nurse entered and administered the punishment. Emma screamed in fury and agony. His heart wrenched. He watched Coco wince then immediately turn into comfort mode. "There you go," she said rubbing the baby's arm. "What a brave girl. All over in no time. You're such a good girl."

Emma quickly became distracted by Coco's words of praise. Her cries subsided and she gave a few extra sobs then sighed.

"You can give her a low dose of baby acetaminophen if she appears uncomfortable," the nurse said. "She's a beautiful baby."

Coco smiled. "Thank you. We think so, too."

They walked out of the office and Benjamin helped Emma into her car seat and escorted Coco into her seat. Emma sucked on her pacifier.

"Poor thing," Coco said. "They go through so much they don't understand."

"Yeah, but it's necessary to keep them alive," Benjamin said. "I would be a rotten father if I didn't protect her against the diseases she could get."

"That's right," Coco agreed. "And you're nowhere near a rotten father." She glanced behind her. "Besides, she's sleeping now."

Benjamin felt something inside him ease. "Good. Just tell me we have that baby Tylenol ready."

"We do," she assured him. "Along with your beer."

The next day, the story hit the Dallas and Houston papers. The weekly Silver City paper wouldn't be far behind. The house phone started ringing. Everyone from newspaper reporters to radio DJs to television reporters wanted to interview Coco about her association with the Devereau family.

Sarah fielded the calls when Coco was busy with Emma, but she was getting antsy by late afternoon. "I don't think I can do another day of this. These phone calls have totally interrupted my cooking and cleaning schedule."

"I'm sorry," Coco said as the phone rang again. "Maybe we should let the calls go to voice mail."

Sarah scoffed and shook her head. "It'll fill up in an hour. I swear, it must be a slow news day for everyone to get worked up over this." She picked up the phone. "Garner Ranch." She paused a few seconds. "Miss Jordan has nothing to say to the press. Pass that along to all your colleagues so they'll stop calling. Goodbye," she said and hung up the phone.

"They'll stop when they figure out I don't know anything about the Devereaux. As long as I continue to be boring, they'll get bored, too," Coco said.

Sarah snorted. "I don't know what you've been drinking, but this is a great story. Pretty girl, orphaned by her adoptive parents, finds out she's a princess—"

"I'm not a princess," Coco said. "I'm a nanny."

"Hmmph," Sarah said. "Try telling that to the reporters."

"I have," Coco said.

The phone rang again and Coco reached for it. She didn't want Sarah getting any more cranky than she already was. "Garner Ranch," she said.

"This is Annie Howell. I'd like to speak with Coco Jordan," the woman said.

Coco sighed. "Speaking."

"Oh, Your Highness. I'm so happy to talk to you," the woman gushed. "I'm the president of the Silver City Ladies Society. We would love for you to come and speak to our group next month."

"Thank you for the kind invitation," Coco said. "But I must tell you that I'm not any kind of highness and I'm very busy working for the Garner household right now."

"But you *are* from royalty," the woman said. "We're so excited to have royalty right here among us."

"But I'm really not royalty. A true royal person is raised to be royal from birth and, trust me, I was not.

I'm sorry I can't help you. Have a good day. Goodbye," she said before the woman could respond.

"These people really don't get it," she murmured.

Emma's cry vibrated through the baby monitor, interrupting her thoughts.

Coco ran upstairs, scooped up Emma, changed her diaper and returned downstairs just as the doorbell rang.

"I'll get it," Sarah said. "Might as well be Grand Central Station in here today with all these interruptions."

Carrying Emma, Coco wandered toward the front room.

Sarah opened the door and looked surprised. "Eunice and Timmy, what brings you here?" she asked, drying her hands on the dish towel she carried.

"May we come in?" the woman outside asked.

"Of course," Sarah said and stepped aside. "What can I do for you, Eunice?"

An older woman with bright red lipstick and unrealistically black hair and a middle-aged man stood inside the door. The woman carried a fruit basket and the man cleared his throat and pressed down his hair.

"We hear you have a princess living in your house and we wanted to welcome her to the neighborhood," Eunice said.

Coco took a silent step backward so she wouldn't be seen.

Sarah paused a half beat then sighed and reached for the basket. "That's nice of you. I'll be sure and tell Coco you dropped by."

"Oh, we were hoping to meet the princess," Eunice said.

"Well, she's busy with the baby right now," Sarah said.

Emma looked down at the dog and made a loud gurgling sound.

"Oh, is that them?"

Emma let out another loud gurgle.

"Coco," Sarah called as if she realized it was no use trying to hide Coco any longer. "You have guests."

Coco entered the room and smiled. "Hello," she said.

"Coco, this is Eunice Chittum and her son, Timmy."

"Tim," the man corrected and cleared his throat.

"Tim," Sarah repeated. "Well, the Chittums have brought you a fruit basket. I'll take it into the kitchen for you."

"Thank you very much," Coco said. "What a nice gift. It's nice to meet you."

"Oh, our pleasure," Eunice gushed and dipped in a curtsey. "Your royalness."

Frustration rippled through Coco. "Oh, no, please don't do that. I'm just Coco Jordan. Really."

"There's no need to be so humble with us. We're very honored to meet you. I especially wanted you to meet Timmy."

"Tim," the man corrected.

"He would be a perfect escort and you should know that he *is* eligible."

"Mother," Timmy said, rubbing at his hair self-consciously.

Coco covered her dismay by shifting Emma to her left hip and extending her hand. "It's nice to meet both of you and so friendly of you to stop by. I wish I could invite you to stay longer, but I need to bathe the baby."

"Oh, of course. We wouldn't dream of imposing, but I do want to leave you with my phone number and Timmy's," the woman said with a bob of her head and handed Coco a floral card with several phone numbers on it. "That last one is Timmy's cell and he always answers. Please call us for anything you might need. Anything at all."

Coco nodded and murmured her thanks again as she closed the door behind them. As soon as they left, she walked to the kitchen where Sarah was cooking. "Just tell me this won't last long," she said over Emma's babbling. Emma was turning into quite the chatty baby. Coco just wished she understood the baby's language.

Sarah shot her a look of sympathy. "Oh, sweetheart, it's just getting started, but maybe if we ask Benjamin to keep it to no visitors for a while, it'll die down faster."

"I hate to be unfriendly," Coco said.

"It's about survival," Sarah said. "We have to survive the incoming."

The phone rang.

"I'll get it," Coco said as Emma continued to babble.

"I'll let you," Sarah said and turned back to stirring her pot.

Coco scooted around the corner to grab the phone

in the den and almost collided with Benjamin. "Oh, I didn't know you were here," she said.

Emma stared at Benjamin's hat and immediately stopped babbling. "She really doesn't like that hat," Sarah muttered.

Rolling his eyes, Benjamin removed it. "I'll get the phone," he said, picking up the receiver.

Coco went after him. "You might not want to do—"

"Garner Ranch," he said and listened. He wrinkled his brow and his face became more and more perturbed. "Wait a minute. Wait, wait a minute. You say you're a DJ at a radio station, and you want to interview Princess Coco Jordan?"

Benjamin glanced at her. She cringed and shook her head.

"She doesn't want to be interviewed," he said and opened his mouth as if he were going to say goodbye. He listened a moment longer and his eyes grew wide with disbelief. "You want to have a reality competition for men who want to marry a princess? That's the most ridiculous thing I've heard in my life—" He broke off and shook his head. "You say you've already got fifty men signed up? I don't care if you've got a million. It's not gonna happen. Ever. Got it? Goodbye."

He hung up the phone and turned to her. "We're gonna need a different strategy."

That night after she put Emma to bed, Coco returned to her bedroom, pulled on a sweatshirt and crept downstairs and out the back door. Her mind whirling a mile a minute, she circled the house. She started out at a fast jog. *What was her blood brother like? Were any of those royals worth knowing? Would any of them consider* her *worth knowing?*

Coco had always dreamed of having brothers and sisters, but her parents had told her she was their everything. In retrospect, she'd felt more than a little pressure from that. She'd always wanted to be the best student, the best artist, the best singer, the best fisher, the best athlete, but in truth, she'd been mostly average.

Oh, she'd been a good speller and her grades had spiked into Dean's List territory every now and then, but along the way, she'd learned that she couldn't be Miss Perfect. And she'd felt a little guilty about it, especially when she'd overheard her parents arguing about money and learned that her parents had spent their life savings to adopt her.

After a time, she'd seen that her requests for a sibling had pained her mother and father, so she'd stopped voicing them. But she'd never stopped wanting a brother or sister or both. And now, she technically had brothers and sisters, all for the taking. Yet she felt as if it were all a bad joke, because she sensed they would regard her as a complication, perhaps a threat.

Which was so ridiculous, because she wasn't a nasty person.

Why couldn't she put this craziness out of her mind? The onslaught of the press didn't help, but she just wished she could turn it all off at night when she went to bed. So far, no luck.

Suddenly, Benjamin appeared by her side, walking with her. “Something bothering you?” he asked in his low drawl.

“It’s been a strange day,” she said a little breathlessly. She inhaled quickly, superaware of his height and muscular frame.

“I’ll say,” he said. “Which bothered you most?” he asked. “Eunice and Timmy? Or the reality competition for your hand in marriage?”

She shot him a dirty look. Ordinarily, she would have been more careful with her reaction to her boss.

He chuckled and gave her a quick elbow. “Looks like you’ve got some extra energy. You need to run,” he said and started to jog.

She couldn’t *not* accept his dare, so she quickened her stride. Coco noticed that Benjamin wasn’t breathing hard. “Were you a football player when you were in high school?”

“And college,” he said. “Why do you ask?”

She shrugged and upped her speed a bit. “Just curious. You’re big, but fit,” she said.

“Big?” he echoed. “I was one of the little guys on the team. But thanks for the compliment. It helps to move around a lot during the day. You should know with all the moving you do for Emma.”

She nodded, concentrating on her pace and breathing.

"You still didn't answer my question about why we're running," he said.

"I don't know why *you* are running," she said.

"Okay, I can settle that. I'm running to keep up with you. Why are you running?"

She ran several more steps. "I don't want to have to deal with all this right now. I just started taking care of Emma. Sarah has been a good sport, but it's not fair to her to have to answer all these crazy phone calls."

"Yeah," he said. "What else?"

She continued jogging then slowed. Then walked. "I don't want to want to meet them," she said, her heart pounding in her chest. "I don't want to care if I ever see one of them face-to-face."

"But you do want to meet them. I would want to," he said, walking beside her.

"You said that before," she said, looking at him.

"Sure. I've got brothers, but I've always known them," he said.

She nodded, taking a deep breath. "The trouble is I don't want to go by myself, and I can't think of anyone to go with me."

"Hmm," he said.

Her heart twisted. "And it's such bad timing."

He rubbed his chin. "It could be worse."

"How?" she asked.

"It's not calving season," he said and met her gaze. "How would you feel about having Emma and me tag along for your trip to Chantaine?"

She gaped at him in amazement. "Are you joking?"

"Don't get the wrong idea. I'm not doing this out of the goodness of my heart," he said. "You're the best one for Emma, and I'll do whatever I have to do to keep you."

Coco blinked while his words sank in. *Allrighty.* She was totally confused for an entire moment, until she realized that Benjamin was still desperate to keep Emma happy, even though his daughter had stopped screaming at the very sight of him.

Chapter Five

The next day, numerous bouquets of flowers, invitations and fruit baskets arrived. The arrivals kept Boomer busy as he tried to greet each deliveryman. Benjamin made a new message for the voice mail and no one was required to pick up the house phone. His men kept all visitors at bay.

Coco breathed a sigh of relief several times throughout the day. Sarah was more relaxed. Even the baby seemed more at ease. The conversation she'd had with Benjamin made her feel alternately uneasy and anxious. Was she really going to Chantaine to meet her half siblings? Had Benjamin really agreed to go with her? And take Emma?

Coco wondered if she'd dreamed it.

"There's no way we can use all this fruit," Sarah said. "Even if we give it to the men."

"Is there someone in the community who could use it?" Coco asked as she slid Emma into her high chair for dinner.

"I could call the church. They might know someone who could take it," Sarah said as she stirred stew on the stove. She gave a slight smile. "It sure has been nice ignoring the phone today, hasn't it?"

"Yes, it has," Coco said as she began to feed Emma. The baby kicked her feet in anticipation of her green beans.

Coco smiled at the baby's puckered lips. "Compared to yesterday, it's been heaven."

"I'm thinking after word of Benjamin's message gets around, the phone won't be ringing near as much tomorrow," Sarah said.

"Why is that?" Coco asked, giving Emma another spoonful of beans.

Sarah chuckled. "It's not exactly a welcoming message."

"I haven't listened to it," Coco said and decided to do that as soon as she finished feeding Emma. "I can't imagine what he said."

"Something along the lines of how you wouldn't be back in touch until after the turn of the next century and trespassers would be prosecuted to the full extent of Texas law," Sarah said, then chuckled. "It's fun when Benjamin gets a little huffy. He's usually not the pushy type. Like his father, he doesn't get riled unless the occasion calls for it."

Sarah made Coco curious. "What was his father like?" Coco asked.

"He was a good, solid man. The ranch was his life. Except for Benjamin, his boys went in different directions. I think Benjamin fought it for a while, but once his father died, he knew his destiny. Except for that crazy affair with Brooke Hastings." Sarah rolled her eyes. "But we all have our foolish moments. This one turned out pretty good when you look at that baby."

Coco smiled at Emma, and Emma gave her a toothless smile in return. Sheer delight rushed through her. "She is adorable, isn't she?"

"When she isn't screaming bloody murder," Sarah said.

"She's still adjusting," Coco said, feeding Emma another spoonful. "What about Benjamin's mother? I haven't heard much about her."

"Well, that's another story," Sarah said as she adjusted the temperature on the burner. "Georgia is her name and you've probably heard she lives in Costa Rica. At the moment, anyway," Sarah said. "Georgia wanted to travel. Benjamin's father, Howard, couldn't and wouldn't. I'm not sure which of those were first."

"It does seem that ranch life is very absorbing."

"It is," Sarah said. "A rancher is married to his ranch and his wife needs to understand that. Georgia went along with it for a long time, but as she and Howard grew older, she wanted them to take vacations. He was resistant. Sometimes, she went on her own. Don't dare repeat this, but their marriage was turbulent because of it."

Coco frowned. "It must have been difficult for both of them if she wanted to travel and he didn't."

Sarah nodded. "Yep. It was. Some people thought she was flighty, but she hung around until her boys were grown."

"What do you think?" Coco asked, knowing Sarah had been employed by the Garners for a long time.

"It's not my place to comment one way or another, but when I saw her, she was a good mother and a good wife. She just got a little wanderlust and some empty-nest syndrome. I know she's grieving now. Traveling won't fill the loss, but it might provide a distraction. Sometimes we all need a distraction."

Coco absorbed Sarah's words. "Very true. You're a wise woman, Sarah."

Sarah smiled, her face creasing in a thousand wrinkles. "Well, thank you very much, your royalness."

Coco laughed. "You know I'll be changing a dirty diaper within thirty minutes."

Sarah nodded. "You're a good girl. You're better than any princess—I'll tell you that much. And you work magic with that baby. It's no wonder Benjamin is willing to do almost anything to protect you. If you ever meet those royal people, you remember they're not better than you. Hear me?"

Coco's heart twisted and her throat swelled with emotion. "I hear you."

"Good, and don't forget what I said," Sarah said.

Later that evening, Benjamin found Coco wading through the flowers and messages she'd received during the day. She pushed a strand of her hair behind her ear and shook her head in frustration. "This is ridiculous," she muttered.

He took a drink of water from his glass. "Long day? You didn't have any visitors, did you?"

She shook her head and looked up at him. "No visitors. Just deliveries and the phone ringing off the hook. It's these crazy requests. These men don't even know me, but they're asking for dates, offering to take me on trips. I feel like I need to put out a press release saying, *I'm broke. You can stop calling now.*"

Benjamin chuckled at her, but at the same time, he felt sorry for her. She hadn't asked for any of this. He admired her for keeping her feet on the ground. Many women would have been demanding a tiara and breakfast in bed if they'd learned they had royal blood in them. But not Coco.

"You don't have to answer them," he said. "These offers you're getting are completely unsolicited."

"I know," she said. "I just wish I wasn't getting them at all." She shrugged. "If I were engaged or married, these men wouldn't be making all these offers."

"True," he said and his mind wandered to his assistant foreman, Jace. Jace would be more than happy to act as Coco's love interest. He scowled at the thought.

"Why are you frowning?" she asked.

"Just thinking," he said and took another drink of water. He walked to the other side of the room then walked back. It wouldn't be a bad idea if Coco had someone looking out for her. She was a smart girl, but probably too sweet and trusting for her own good. If people knew they would have to deal with a protective man in her life, they might be less likely to try to take advantage of her.

He watched as Coco opened another card. She sighed.

He gave in to his curiosity. "What's that one?"

"A mother wants money for her sick child," she said, her voice miserable.

"It could be valid, but it may not be," he said.

She looked at him in shock. "You mean, you think someone would lie about that?"

He nodded. "Oh, yeah. Especially in this situation."

"That's—that's—horrible," she said. "I mean, what if I *were* a real princess and I got these kinds of requests?

"They would be screened by your staff," he said.

"I don't have staff," she said. *"I am staff."* She opened another envelope attached to a bouquet of roses. "Oh, goody, another invitation. This one from David Gordan in Dallas inviting me to a Christmas ball?" She lifted her hands helplessly.

He frowned. The name rang a bell. "Let me see that," he said and she handed him the typed note. "David Gordan. That's my stockbroker's son." He shook his head. "This is out of control." He sighed. "Well, damn. I guess I'm gonna have to be your fiancé."

Coco dropped her jaw. "What?"

"It won't be real," he said quickly, as much for himself as for her. After the debacle of his relationship with Brooke, the idea of an engagement nearly gave him hives. "It's just for the sake of appearances until the insanity dies down. This way it won't look like you're all alone and ready to have someone take advantage of you. If someone approaches you, they'll have to deal with me, too."

Her eyebrows furrowed. "I'm stronger than I seem," she said.

"I know you're strong. After what you went through for your mom and helping Emma to settle down, I know you're strong. But it's gotta be damn tiring to feel like you've always got to be on guard."

Coco sighed and her shoulders slumped. "You're right about that." She met his gaze with a wince. "Are you sure you don't mind doing this?"

"It's just for a little while," he said. "You mentioned that a fiancé would fix things a few minutes ago. I had to run it through my brain. It seems like the right thing to do."

She gave a slow nod and bit her lip. "Hmm. But it would cut into your dating time," she ventured.

He laughed. "That's not a big focus at the moment," he said.

"It would be a huge relief for me," she admitted. "If you're sure you don't mind. And we'll break it off the second you feel inconvenienced," she said with a firm nod.

"All right," he said. "I'll give Sarah the news in the morning. Should be all over the country by lunchtime."

Her lips twitched. "She seems pretty discreet to me."

"Trust me, if I tell her that she can share the information, she'll take off like a runaway horse. And she will love having this kind of scoop."

"Are you going to tell her the truth?"

He shook his head. "No one except you and I can know the truth. That's the only way it will work."

Coco took a deep breath and squished her eyes together as if she was preparing to take a jump into deep water. "Okay," she said and opened her eyes. "Let's do it."

Two days later, Benjamin, Emma and Coco boarded a flight with a connection in England that would land in Chantaine. Coco was so anxious that she feared she would explode during the flight. Plus she was hyperaware of Benjamin now that they were supposedly engaged. She noticed that he treated her a little differently in front of people. Even in front of Sarah, he'd touched her arm and put his hand at her waist a couple of times. It had caught her off guard, but she realized they needed to appear as if they were romantically involved. She hadn't considered that when he'd offered to be her fiancé.

Coco had thought Benjamin was attractive before the engagement thing, but she'd pushed it aside and focused on Emma's adjustment. She would have to be blind to be totally immune to his tall, wide-shouldered frame and rugged masculine features. Now she was going to have to work twice as hard not to give in to her attraction to him. The fact that she'd been sitting mere inches away from him for hours wasn't helping her, either.

"Go to sleep," he said, cracking open one of his eyes.

"But Emma," she said, even though the baby was so deep in sleep she was drooling on Coco's sweater.

"She'll let us know if she wants something. Here," he said, extending his arms. "I'll take her."

Emma was out, so she probably wouldn't wake up even with the transition.

"Come on," he said. "You're wound way too tight. You need to close your eyes for a few moments."

Coco gingerly handed the baby to Benjamin, and saw that Emma barely stirred. She nestled against her daddy's chest and gave a soft baby sigh. The sight made Coco smile. "Maybe something good will come of this trip after all," she said.

"Go to—"

"Okay, okay," Coco said. "I'll rest my eyes, but I won't fall asleep."

One moment she was thinking about Benjamin. Then next she was thinking about meeting her half brothers and half sisters. The next moment, she heard a baby babbling. Blinking her eyes, she glanced over at Benjamin.

Emma, who was sitting on his lap, was having a baby conversation with him.

Shaking off her sleep, Coco stretched and smoothed over her hair. "How long was I asleep?"

He glanced at his wristwatch. "About two hours," he said.

"You're joking," she said.

"Nope," he said. "Emma woke up and started screaming bloody murder, so I had to walk her up and down the aisle."

Chagrined, she bit her lip. "And I slept through her screaming?"

"No," he said and his mouth stretched into a sly grin. "I was joking about that part, but I did walk her up and down the aisle a few times. She's gonna be a talker, isn't she?"

"I think so," Coco said, smiling at Emma and him. "I'll change her diaper. I'm sure she's due."

An hour later, they landed in Heathrow and grabbed a bite to eat. Soon enough, it was time to board the flight for Chantaine. Coco's nerves returned. She watched out the window as they drew close to the Chantaine airport. The island country was beautiful. The white sandy beach around the island was broken by jutting outcrops of rocks. The vivid blue of ocean contrasted sharply with the shore. She couldn't believe that she was connected to the island in any way. As the jet managed a three-point landing, she felt herself swell with anticipation. Soon, very soon, she would meet her half brothers and half sisters.

Benjamin carried Emma as they departed the plane, and after they collected their luggage, they left the airport to find a limo waiting for them. Coco met Benjamin's gaze. "Is this a big mistake?"

He chuckled. "We'll find out."

She smiled. "Thanks a lot."

"You wanted to come here," he pointed out.

"I know. I know," she said.

"Just think of it as a nice vacation," he said and leaned his head back against the seat.

"I'll try," she said and took a deep breath.

"Do you think they'll like me?" she asked him.

"If they don't, they're nuts," he said.

"Why?" she asked then shook her head. "Don't answer that. I'm just being weird and insecure."

"You're a damn good woman—princess or not," Benjamin said. "I'm not flattering you. Just telling the truth."

"Thank you," she said, but she was still nervous. "This is a little crazy."

"Roll with it," he told her. "When have you ever visited a Mediterranean island where the ruler was determined to meet and greet you?"

She took a deep breath. "Okay. I'll work on it. Our Emma sure was a good traveler, wasn't she?" she said in a low voice.

"Yeah, we'll see what happens tonight," he said. "The time change could be hell for all of us."

Coco was surprised when the limo drove past the palace gates. "I thought they would put us in a hotel outside the palace complex," she said to Benjamin.

"You underestimated yourself," he said.

She struggled with doubt. "We'll see."

Moments later, the chauffeur unloaded the luggage and carted it to a small villa with three bedrooms. Emma began to wake up as they stepped inside. Coco jiggled her as she walked into the villa.

The chauffeur guided her and Benjamin through the small building. "A cook is available to you. A nanny is available to you," he said. "Whatever you need, just dial this code," he said and wrote down a series of numbers. "Is there anything you need right now?" he asked.

Coco glanced at Benjamin.

"A few sandwiches would be nice," he said. "We need a little rest. Don't expect any of us to make an appearance before tomorrow."

The chauffeur nodded. "As you wish, sir."

The man left and Coco and Benjamin looked at the den of the villa. "This is nice," she said.

"Not bad. And we have a cook and a nanny at our disposal," Benjamin added.

"Yeah. Good luck with that nanny thing with Emma," she said and jiggled Emma again.

"You never know," he said. "She let me hold her for hours today."

"True," Coco said. "Sometimes babies grow and change when they visit different environments and have new experiences. So we'll see. Let's start with a blanket on the floor so she can stretch out and wiggle."

"Works for me," he said and pulled a blanket out of his backpack. He put it on the floor and she placed Emma on it. The baby immediately began to lift her head and feet. And wiggle. Emma made groaning sounds as if she were doing an aerobic workout.

"Go, girl," Benjamin said.

Coco laughed at his low-voiced cheer. "I just hope she'll expend enough energy to sleep in an hour or so."

"If she doesn't, we'll take turns," he said.

Coco wandered through the villa again, noticing the fine linens on the beds and in the bathrooms. "I'm surprised at how nice it is."

"What did you think? They would put you in the dungeon?" he asked.

"No," she said. "Well, maybe. After all, I'm the illegitimate spawn."

He chuckled and shook his head. "I know this is strange for you, but you may as well roll with it. In the scheme of things, how many people get a call telling them their father was a ruling prince?"

"True," she said. "I'll work on it. Which bedroom do you want?"

"Any room where my dear daughter is not sleeping," he said.

She laughed. "The good news is she can have her

own bedroom and I brought monitors so we know if she's crying."

"Works for me. I could use a beer. You could use some wine. Let me see if I can find something for both of us," he said and opened the refrigerator. "We're in luck. German beer," he said with a snicker. "White wine?" he asked her.

"I'm good with water. The flight was exhausting," she said. "I need to be ready when Emma wakes up after we put her to bed."

"You could call the nanny they offered," Benjamin said.

"Not tonight. Maybe another time," Coco said.

Moments later, sandwiches were delivered and Coco devoured hers. She diapered Emma, put her in the crib and fell asleep in the bedroom next to the nursery. With her clothes on.

Dead to the world, Coco awakened to the sound of a baby screaming. Blindly, she scrambled out of bed and rushed out of her bedroom toward the screaming. She bumped into a large, strong frame.

"Benjamin?" she murmured.

"Yeah," he muttered in return.

She stumbled into the nursery and pulled Emma up into her arms. "You're okay," Coco cooed.

Emma screamed in protest and Coco cuddled the baby closer. "You're okay," Coco said.

In short order, Emma calmed down. "Bet you need a diaper change," Coco said. "I can do that in no time."

Finding a flat surface, Coco set the baby down. Emma fussed, but Coco quickly changed her wet diaper and picked her up.

"Good girl," Coco said.

"That was fast," Benjamin said.

"It's all instinct when you do it every day," she said. "She's awake now. It may take a while for her to go back to sleep."

"I can stay up," he offered.

She shook her head. "I want you awake when I'm not," she said. "I'll take this shift."

"You're sure?" he asked.

"More than," she said. "Besides, you're due the rest since you walked her up and down the aisle while she was screaming on the plane," she said, lightly mocking him.

He chuckled. "Yeah. Well, let me know if you need me," he said and gently touched the tip of her nose. "Tomorrow's going to be a busy day for you."

Her stomach danced with nerves. "We'll see."

The next morning, a staff member from the kitchen delivered a basket of bread, butter and jellies along with coffee and hot tea. "This is breakfast?" Benjamin said, biting into a roll. "At least there's coffee," he said and poured a cup.

"Maybe this is all they eat for breakfast," she said as she gave Emma her bottle. "Or they're hoping they can starve us into leaving early."

He tossed her a sly look, and it occurred to her that the man was too good-looking for her own good anytime day or night. “No need for paranoia yet. You haven't even met them,” he said. “You look tired. Did Emma go back to sleep?” he asked.

“After about an hour, but then I was wound up and couldn't. I think my internal clock is messed up.”

He nodded. “Plus you're meeting your royal relations today.”

“True,” she said and the phone rang.

“I'll get it,” he said and picked it up. “Benjamin Garner,” he said. “Yes, Miss Jordan is here.” He nodded. “Afternoon tea,” he said, waggling his eyebrows in Coco's direction. “And this morning, a royal representative would like to take Miss Jordan for a tour of the palace grounds.”

“What time?” she asked because she hadn't showered yet and knew she looked like something the cat dragged in.

“What time?” he repeated and waited for the answer. “In an hour?”

She nodded. “Yes,” she said and put Emma on her shoulder to burp her.

Chapter Six

Promptly one hour later, a knock sounded on the front door of the villa. With Emma in one arm, Benjamin opened the door to a slim, middle-aged, balding man wearing a suit.

"Hello," the man said, his gaze sweeping the small foyer. "I'm Peter Bernard for Miss Coco Jordan. I presume you are Mr. Garner," Peter said. "You and the baby are more than welcome to join us."

"I'd like for her not to be distracted by the baby during the tour," Benjamin said, towering over the man as he extended his hand. "Miss Jordan is very important to me. I trust you'll take good care of her."

Coco grabbed her jacket and walked toward the door. Benjamin caught her arm before she could leave and she met his gaze. "Have fun, sweetheart. Emma and I will be waiting for you," he said and lowered his head to kiss her.

Coco stared at him for a long moment, stunned that he'd *kissed* her, then she reminded herself that this was part of their ruse. She finally managed to take a breath and nodded. "Thanks. I hope she'll take a little nap. I'll see you later, um, *honey*." She nearly choked on the word. This was going to be more difficult than she'd anticipated.

"Miss Jordan," the man at the door prompted.

"Yes," she said, relieved to have her attention diverted from Benjamin. "Mr. Bernard."

He nodded and escorted her to a car parked in front of the villa. "We shall tour the grounds first and I'll provide you with a history of the Devereau family," he said as the driver opened the door for her and Mr. Bernard.

"Although our gardens and vegetation are always lovely here in Chantaine, unfortunately, due to the time of the year, most of our flowers are not in full bloom. As you can see, however, we have several green courtyards that provide the royal family with opportunities for moments to ponder and escape the pressures of their responsibilities."

Coco drank in the sight of the lush, green palace grounds. She could only imagine how stunning they would be with colorful flowers and foliage. As Mr. Bernard continued to give her a running commentary on the various buildings, including guest cottages, staff quarters and stables, she wondered what it would be like to grow up in a place like this. She thought of her own childhood home in a rural town in Texas and smiled.

"Do you have fishing ponds?" she asked.

Mr. Bernard blinked at her. "Fishing ponds?"

"Yes. Large ponds where you can swim and fish," she said.

Mr. Bernard gave a slight smile. "We have a pool and ocean for swimming. Likewise, the royal yacht can be used for fishing expeditions. There are a few stocked ponds on the property that feature mostly garibaldi fish and carp. Do you have more questions?"

She shook her head. "Not right now."

"Very well, we shall now proceed to the palace," he said.

Mr. Bernard began to share the history of the Deveraux family and Chantaine. The family, of course, went back centuries and representatives of the crown had conducted a series of negotiations with both France and Italy in order for the royal family to remain in power and for Chantaine to maintain its independence.

"Some men are born to rule and some are determined to make a difference. Chantaine is proud that with this new generation, the royal family actively seeks to improve the quality of life for all of Chantaine's people. Within the last several years, His Royal Highness, Stefan, has invited a limited number of cruise ships to our port. He and the rest of the royal family have instituted art, music and film events with percentages donated to Chantaine's charities. And, of course, Her Highness Bridget married a highly credentialed American doctor, who now serves as our chief medical officer. Prince Stefan is always looking for ways to improve Chantaine."

The car slowed to a stop in front of the grand palace entrance. White columns rose several stories high. A man in uniform stood at the front door. The driver ushered her out of the car and she joined Mr. Bernard as the huge heavy door opened to a grand two-story foyer with curving staircases and marble floors. Above her hung several chandeliers.

"Wow," she whispered.

Mr. Bernard continued his discourse as he led her throughout the main floor of the palace, which held numerous meeting rooms, two ballrooms and several nooks with antique furniture where someone could look out the window and enjoy the sight of the palace grounds. As her guide commented on the origin of the architecture of the palace, she couldn't contain her curiosity any longer.

"What was he like?" she asked. "Prince Edward?"

Mr. Bernard seemed slightly taken aback. "Prince Edward was a sword master. His passion was yachting and he was loyal in his duties as prince. He graduated from university in France and provided Chantaine with an excellent heir, along with a progeny that are a delight to our citizens."

"And his—" she paused, wanting to repeat the word

he'd used, though it wasn't one she would dream of choosing "—his progeny. What are they like?"

"As I said, they are delightful."

But that didn't answer her question.

Coco ate half her sandwich with Emma on her lap while Benjamin wolfed down the meal delivered from the palace kitchen. He eyed her remaining half sandwich.

She shoved her plate toward him. "Take it. I'm not going to eat it. I have formal tea in a short while. Can we look that up on Google? I've never had a formal tea before."

"You're sure?" he asked, staring at her sandwich.

"I'm sure," she said and shoved her plate toward him.

He immediately scooped up her half sandwich. "Did you get any real information?" he asked before he took a bite.

"He was very nice and informative, but when I asked what the royal family was like, he said *delightful.*"

He scowled. "No one is always delightful. He's a PR guy. You'll get a better feel for this after this afternoon."

"But I'm nervous now," she confessed. "I've *never* had a formal tea before and certainly never with royals. I really need to check Google. Am I supposed to curtsey?"

"It's a choice. You're not one of their subjects," he said. "You're not a citizen of their country."

"True," she said, feeling conflicted. "I just want to be respectful."

He snorted. "Let them be respectful to you."

His response made her smile.

Emma waved toward the plate she'd shoved in Benjamin's direction and protested as if she wanted what was on his plate.

"Uh-oh," he said.

"Yes. We have jars ready for her. As soon as you finish, can you give her some food while I look up *high tea* on the internet?"

He chuckled. "Yeah, I'm there," he said, reaching for Emma.

Emma hesitated.

"He's got the food," Coco said in a low voice and gave Emma a squeeze before she passed the baby to him.

"And that baby food is where?" he asked as Emma began to squawk.

"I'll get it," Coco said and found a jar in a backpack. "Here," she said, giving him a jar of strained peas.

He made a face. "This didn't end well the last time I fed her strained peas."

"Stop when she starts to spit. Don't continue to put food in when she is spitting it out," she said. "It's pretty logical."

He frowned. "Easy for you to say. You do this all the time."

"This is your opportunity to bond with your daughter," she said.

Emma began to fuss and lift her arms toward Coco. "Oops, I'll go into a different room and try to find out more about an afternoon tea. May I use your tablet?" Coco asked.

"Go right ahead," he said.

Emma let out a loud scream of protest that tugged at Coco's heart, but she forced herself to close the door behind her. She suffered during the next couple moments while Emma loudly voiced her displeasure. Finally, the baby quieted, and Coco's stomach unknotted just a bit. She was still tense about meeting her half siblings.

Pulling out the tablet, she ran a search on afternoon tea and scanned for proper etiquette. *No circular stirring. Move spoon from six o'clock position to twelve o'clock position. Never put your napkin in the seat. Don't slice your scone....*

Coco made a face. She didn't even like scones. She continued to cram for the tea when a knock sounded on the door. Her stomach jolted into her throat and she jumped to her feet.

Taking a deep breath, she walked through the kitchen where Emma grinned at her. Peas were smeared on her cheeks and in her hair. "I think she's done," she said in a low voice to Benjamin.

"Think so?" he said in a dry tone. "I made the mistake of giving her the spoon."

Coco watched Emma bang the spoon on the tray then toss it onto the floor. She winced. "Bad precedent. We'll need to distract her during her next mealtime."

Another knock sounded and Coco met Benjamin's gaze. He rose to walk her to the door. "Just remember what I told you. Even that Emily Post woman says Americans should not bow or curtsey to anyone."

"I'm pretty sure Emily Post never wrote a column about this particular situation," she muttered and opened the door.

Benjamin grabbed her arm and lowered his head to press his mouth against hers. "I've got your back," he said.

His reassurance gave her a warm feeling. "Thanks," she said and joined Mr. Bernard for the second time that day.

Mr. Bernard prepped her for the tea during the short drive to the palace. "I'll introduce each of the princesses to you individually. Prince Stefan will stop in later, due to his work schedule. Come this way," he said and guided her down the marble hallway to a small room furnished with a lush wool carpet, antique furniture and a small table set with a sterling tea set, china teacups and saucers, small plates and a small tower of the scones she was not supposed to slice, along with jellies and other treats.

Mr. Bernard stood next to the door while Coco waited and walked around the room. She didn't want to be suspicious, but she couldn't help wondering if he were remaining in the room because he thought she might lift a souvenir and try to pocket it. The notion made her fume. She might not have been raised in a palace, but she'd been taught the difference between right and wrong.

Coco took a deep breath and chided herself. *Be positive.*

Suddenly, she heard footsteps and three women walked through the doorway. Mr. Bernard bowed to each of them. After studying their photographs on the internet, Coco could name each of them. The blonde was Princess Fredericka. The stylish brunette was Princess Bridget and the woman with the sweet face and wild hair and who also appeared to be sporting a baby bump was Princess Phillipa.

"Princess Fredericka, may I present Miss Coco Jordan," Mr. Bernard said.

In the interest of erring on the side of politeness, Coco attempted a curtsey and briefly bowed her head.

Fredericka extended her hand. "My pleasure to meet you," she said and stepped aside for Mr. Bernard to introduce Princess Bridget. She also followed with, "My pleasure to meet you."

The icy formality strained her nerves as she prepared for her third curtsey. "Princess Phillipa, I present Miss Coco Jordan."

Princess Phillipa took Coco's hand with both of hers. "My pleasure to meet you. Thank you for coming such a long distance to meet us. Shall we sit and drink tea?"

Coco breathed a slight sigh of relief. At least Princess Phillipa seemed friendly.

A server appeared and poured the tea, asking each person. "Sugar or cream?"

"Just sugar, please," Coco said. "Thank you very much."

She watched the princesses do the vertical stirring motion she'd read on the internet and followed their example. A long silence followed.

The princesses exchanged expressions with each other. Bridget set down her teacup. "I understand you live in Texas. As you probably know, our family has associations with several Texans. My sister Princess Valentina lives in Texas with her husband and daughter, and my husband is originally from Texas. Do you like it there?"

"I don't really know anything else," Coco said. "I've lived there my entire life and haven't traveled all that much. My experience is that there are a lot of good people in Texas. Because of that, I consider myself pretty lucky."

Bridget nodded and glanced at Fredericka. "Texas has such charm. I'm not sure I could endure your summers. How do you do it?"

"Air-conditioning and iced tea and lemonade," she said.

Phillipa laughed. "That sounds like something Eve would say. Eve is our brother Prince Stefan's wife. She's also from Texas. I'm not sure how much Mr. Bernard has shared with you or what you may have gleaned from the internet about the family."

"Mr. Bernard gave me a tour this morning and gave me a brief history lesson on Chantaine and the Devereau family, but it was so much information, I may not be able to pass the quiz if I have to take it this afternoon," she confessed.

Bridget's lips lifted in a half smile that she quickly hid with her teacup. "Tell us about yourself."

Coco immediately felt at a loss. "Well, as you know, I'm from Texas. I'm studying for a degree in early childhood education. Well, I *was* studying, but my mother became ill." She noticed that she was cupping her teacup and remembered that was a no-no, so she put one of her hands in her lap.

"We're sorry for your loss," Phillipa said. "My husband has recently been through a similar experience with his mother."

"Oh, I'm sorry. My sympathies to both of you," Coco said.

"Did I understand correctly that you are working as a nanny?" Bridget asked.

"Yes," Coco said. "For Benjamin Garner's daughter, Emma. She's adorable."

"How old is she?" Bridget asked.

"Only five months old, but quite verbal."

Bridget's eyes rounded in surprise. "She's already talking?"

"In her special language," Coco said. "She's quite the magpie."

Phillipa laughed. "When you're not taking care of Emma, what do you like to do?"

"I have to be honest, most of my time has been spent

helping Emma adjust to living with her father. Emma's mother died suddenly less than two months ago. But when I get the chance, I like to fish."

All three of the princesses stared at her silently, and Coco wondered if she'd overshared.

"Fish?" Fredericka echoed.

Coco nodded. "With a pole and a worm or crawdads."

"Eve would love this," Bridget muttered under her breath. "She already thinks we're a bunch of sissies, so—"

The door to the room opened and Mr. Bernard announced, "His Royal Highness, Prince Stefan."

Coco's mind went blank, but she noticed the princesses rose, so she did the same. Clumsily. She knocked over her teacup, spilling the brown liquid onto the exquisite tablecloth.

"Oh, no! I'm so sorry. I—" She reached for her napkin and began to mop up the liquid. "How will you ever get this tea out of this beautiful material? I—"

"Miss Coco Jordan," another male voice said.

Coco glanced up to meet Prince Stefan's gaze. He didn't look friendly. She gave a quick curtsey, on the wrong foot, and dipped her head.

Prince Stefan extended his hand and she rose. "It is our pleasure to meet you. I trust Mr. Bernard has taken good care of you," he said.

"Yes, thank you."

"I must leave due to a meeting this afternoon. Please don't hesitate to call Mr. Bernard for anything you may need during your stay. Have a good day to all of you," he said, glancing at his sisters and he left the room.

Coco vaguely remembered that she was supposed to curtsey again, so she did, using the correct foot this time. As soon as the prince left, the servers changed the tablecloth in record time. Self-conscious, Coco glanced toward the princesses. Their expressions suddenly seemed cool and remote. Coco would almost swear someone had turned the temperature in the room down to freezing.

Sinking carefully into her chair, Coco pressed her lips together and made herself smile. None of the princesses returned her forced grimace. A server asked her if she would like more tea and she shook her head. She didn't want to ruin any more antique linens.

Silence permeated the room like the most stifling heat and humidity in July. Coco was at a loss as to what to say, and it appeared the princesses felt no need to chat. She wondered if they were truly that upset about her spilling tea.

A clock sounded three times. Fredericka glanced at her watch and stood. Her sisters followed. Coco quickly rose to her feet.

"We've kept you long enough," Fredericka said. "It was a pleasure to meet you and we hope you'll enjoy your visit to our lovely country."

Blinking from the abrupt ending to the visit, Coco dipped a few times. The princesses exited the room and Mr. Bernard appeared. "I shall escort you to your villa now," he said.

Her mind whirled during the few moments it took to ride to the villa. *Was that it?* she wondered. She'd flown halfway around the world to have tea with her so-called half sisters and a few seconds with her so-called half brother.

She'd told herself to expect nothing. Her stomach began to turn and her heart hurt. Locking her fists together, she lectured herself. *Do not get upset. Do not get upset.*

Mr. Bernard ushered her out of the car. She felt him watching her as she walked toward the front door.

"I'm not disappointed," she whispered to herself. "I'm not disappointed. I'm not—"

The front door opened before she'd barely touched it and Benjamin—strong, wonderful Benjamin—studied her face. "How'd it go?" he asked.

Coco burst into tears.

"Not great," Benjamin muttered and gently pulled Coco into the small den. He helped her onto the love seat as she continued to cry.

"I—shouldn't—have—" She broke off and sobbed again.

The sound made his gut twist. Plus, he was starting to get real concerned that she would hyperventilate. "Hey," he said, taking her shoulders. "Take a breath."

She opened her mouth as if she were trying to comply, but another sob escaped. "I'm sorry," she managed. "I haven't—"

"Take a breath," he told her. "Really." He cupped her face. "Close your eyes. And breathe."

She closed her eyes and drew in a shaky breath. She shuddered as she exhaled.

"Another one," he told her.

She breathed again and her sigh was a little less shaky. "I'm sorry. I can't remember the last time I cried this much."

"Then I guess you've been holding it in. If you're okay, I'll get you some water," he said.

She nodded and rubbed at her wet cheeks. "Just embarrassed."

"Don't be," he said and got up to get her a glass of water. "You're in one hell of a strange situation."

Returning, he held the glass to her lips and noticed how plump and pink her mouth was. She sipped the water then took the glass with her own hands. "Thanks." She took another sip and another deep breath and shook her head. "I just feel so stupid."

"Why?"

"I don't know what I was thinking. I kept telling myself and you that they wouldn't have any interest in me, but some stupid part of me must have hoped they would." She closed her eyes. "It's not that I really believed there was any chance for a real sister-sister or sister-brother kind of relationship. I just hoped it would be a little more friendly."

"What did they do?"

"Nothing terrible," she said. "They were just horribly polite. The prince came into the room where we were having tea and I spilled my tea all over this beautiful tablecloth. I wondered if that was why they acted so cold after he arrived. He was only there for about a half minute." She shook her head in confusion. "Before that, Bridget and Phillipa were almost nice. They even smiled a couple times and laughed."

Benjamin frowned. Why would the royal chicks turn suddenly mean? "Did Prince Stuffy say anything to his sisters when he was there?"

"Stefan," Coco corrected, but laughed. "Never thought of that about his name, but—"

"Did he say anything to his sisters?" he repeated.

She shook her head. "No. He kinda glared at them, but he didn't say anything."

"Hmm," Benjamin said, wondering if the way the royals had behaved toward Coco was all part of a plan.

"What are you thinking?" she asked.

"Just thinking," he said.

"Well, I don't have to think about this situation one more minute," she said. "I'm ready to leave now."

Emma let out a cry from the room where she was sleeping. "Oh," Coco said. "I should get her. I hope I didn't wake her."

"Probably not. She's been asleep for a while," he said and thought about Coco's situation with the Devereaux. He hadn't expected them to fall all over themselves welcoming her, but something about it didn't smell right to Benjamin.

An hour later, after Coco gave Emma a bottle and her dinner, she put the baby on a big blanket on the floor of the den. Benjamin noticed Coco pacing restlessly. She was still upset about the Devereaux. He'd come up with a plan of his own, but he didn't want to tell her about it quite yet.

"It's still light out. You want to take her for a little stroll?" he asked.

Coco nodded, her face easing with relief. "Great idea. Do you want to go?"

"I think I'll stay inside. I need to go over some updates from the foreman," he said.

"Okay," she said and put a light jacket and a little hat on Emma. "We won't be gone long," she said and stopped suddenly. "Thank you for putting up with me this afternoon."

The expression in her blue eyes made his chest knot. "It wasn't anything. I just want you to feel better," he said and squeezed her shoulder.

She rose on tiptoe and surprised the heck out of him when she brushed her soft lips across his jaw. "It was a big something to me," she countered, then fastened the baby in the stroller and left.

Benjamin rubbed his jaw at the strange sensation where she'd kissed him. He wondered if the rest of her was as soft as her lips. He wondered what her lips would feel like on his body. He wondered what kind of sounds she would make if he kissed her and touched her all over.

His body heated and he shook his head at himself.

Crazy, he told himself. He had more important things to think about than the fact that he hadn't been with a woman in too long. If there was one woman he shouldn't even be thinking about taking to his bed, it was Coco. She was too important to him because of Emma. Coco was off-limits and he was damn determined to make sure he didn't forget that.

Benjamin walked toward the telephone in the villa and picked it up. He dialed the number for Mr. Bernard, who picked up after the first ring.

"Bernard. May I help you?"

"Yes, you may. I need to speak with Stefan Devereau."

Silence followed. "Pardon," Bernard said. "To whom am I speaking?"

"This is Benjamin Garner, Miss Coco Jordan's fiancé."

Bernard cleared his throat. "Mr. Garner, I'm afraid it will be impossible to arrange an audience with the prince. His schedule is arranged months in advance."

"I don't want an audience. I want a man-to-man chat," he said. "You can tell Stefan that the Devereaux family will be facing a public relations nightmare if he can't find time to talk with me. Understand?"

Bernard cleared his throat. "I will relay your message, Mr. Garner."

"You do that," Benjamin said and hung up the phone.

Chapter Seven

The phone in the villa rang two hours later. Benjamin picked up quickly since Coco had fallen asleep on the sofa.

"Benjamin Garner," he said in a low voice.

"Mr. Garner, this is Prince Stefan's assistant. He will see you for fifteen minutes this evening. Mr. Bernard will pick you up within five minutes."

Benjamin didn't like dancing to someone else's tune, but this wasn't about him. He was taking care of Coco. Even the phone hadn't awakened her. "I can do that," he said and hung up the phone.

He glanced in the den and saw that Coco was still asleep. Poor thing was completely tuckered out. He grabbed the baby monitor, put it next to her on the end table, scrawled a note about taking a walk, and went out the front door. Seconds later, the car slowed to a stop and Bernard popped out.

"Mr. Garner," he said and opened the door. "I'll brief you on proper etiquette with the Prince."

"No need," Benjamin said and got in the car. "He's not my prince."

"But, sir," Mr. Bernard sputtered. "I have instructions. I must brief you."

"Do what you have to do, but I won't be listening. I've got more important things to think about," Benjamin said. "I'll take responsibility for my own actions. I always have."

Mr. Bernard hesitated a half beat. "Very well, sir. The first rule is that you never turn your back on a royal and..."

Benjamin clicked Mr. Bernard's voice to the off position and planned his strategy with Stefan. Just a few moments later, he was led through a side door and upstairs to the second floor. He passed a plainclothes security man and was stopped outside a door by another security man.

"Monsieur, I will now inspect you before your meeting with His Highness," the man said.

Benjamin lifted his hands. He didn't need a gun in this situation. He knew his biggest weapon was tarnishing the precious image of the Devereaux. Seconds later, he was led into a large office furnished with rich woods and leather. He noticed a child's toy on the desk and was surprised. A photograph of a woman with dark hair and laughing eyes graced the mantel behind him, along with a picture of a little girl with ringlet curls and blue eyes.

Benjamin lifted his eyebrows, speculating. So maybe Stefan was human after all. A few moments later, a man entered the room. "His Royal Highness, Stefan Devereaux."

Benjamin stood as the man who was Stefan entered the room. Tall with black hair, cold eyes and a frown, he stalked into the room. "Mr. Garner," Stefan said more than asked.

"Yes. Evenin'," he said and waited for Stefan to take a seat at his desk before he sat down.

"My assistant tells me that you delivered a threat regarding your intent to attack the reputation of my family," Stefan said.

"That's a bit overdramatic," Benjamin said. "I just thought you would want to know what kind of impression your family is making on your newly revealed relative. Coco gets tons of calls every day from the media. All she needs to do is tell the truth about her visit and it won't be good for the royal family."

"What more does she want? She enjoyed tea with my sisters. I made a personal appearance," Stefan said, his jaw tightening. "Perhaps this is a monetary issue. Very well, how much does she want?"

Benjamin scowled in return. "That's insulting. Anyone ever tell you that you could use a little more compassion?"

The man at the door moved forward. "I shall remove Mr. Garner at once."

Stefan waved the man aside. "No, Peter. I'll handle this." He leaned forward. "What exactly does Miss Jordan want?"

Benjamin sighed. "This may be difficult for you, but try to imagine this. You're an only child. You're adopted. Your father is dead. Your mother just died of a terminal illness. You're all alone in the world with no relatives. What would you want?"

Silence followed. For three seconds. A woman burst into the office. "What are you doing working this late at night?" the woman demanded.

It took a moment, but Benjamin recognized her from the photograph, except her face was pale and she looked ill. The man at the door began to apologize.

Stefan immediately rose and crossed the room to take the woman in his arms. "Eve, you shouldn't be up. You've had a rough day. Go back to bed. I'll be there soon."

The woman frowned and glanced at Benjamin, who had also risen.

He gave a nod. "Ma'am."

She narrowed her eyes and returned her gaze to Stefan. "He's from Texas." She paused a half beat and her eyes widened in realization. "He's with Coco Jordan. Is she here? How did I miss her?"

"I told you I would handle this. You weren't feeling

well, so Bridget, Phillipa and Fredericka had tea with her today."

"Tea?" Eve echoed in disdain. "You gave a girl from Texas tea? And I bet it wasn't iced." She took a deep breath. "What's going on?"

"We can discuss this later," Stefan said.

"That's fine," she said. "In the meantime, I'd like to meet a fellow Texan." She moved toward Benjamin. "Hello. I'm Eve Devereaux," she said, extending her hand.

"My pleasure," Benjamin said. "I'm Benjamin Garner. Hate to see your sleep disturbed. I'm sure your husband and I can finish our talk."

"Bourbon or whiskey?" she asked with a faint smile and sank into a chair.

"Eve," Stefan said. "I insist that you return to our quarters."

"Only if you promise I can meet with both Benjamin and Coco tomorrow. And only if you promise to give Benjamin his choice of liquor. You must also take a drink with him," she said.

"As you request," he said, his mouth tight with impatience.

"And," she said.

"And that's enough," he said firmly.

She smiled and rose. "Had to try," she said and pursed her lips in a smooch before she exited the room.

Stefan gave a heavy sigh. "Please be seated. Peter, please get Mr. Garner something to drink."

The man stepped next to Stefan's desk. "Yes, sir. What would you like?"

"Whiskey will do," Benjamin said.

"I'll take the same," Stefan said. He met Benjamin's gaze. "Now that you've gained my wife's attention, I should warn you that I'll be ruthless if you take advantage of her kindness."

Benjamin lifted the glass of perfect single-barrel whiskey in a salute to Stefan. "Glad to hear it, Your Highness. Wouldn't want it any other way."

Stefan knocked back his whiskey. "Very well. There will be a family visit tomorrow. One of the advisors will also convey Miss Jordan's financial inheritance. I should warn you that the amount is meager. These days, royals earn their pay and are encouraged to live on the palace grounds."

Benjamin nodded. Although he would protect Coco's financial interests, he knew what she wanted most. "Make it as friendly as you can. You met her. She's no shark." He stood, leaving the rest of his drink on the desk. "I think we're about done. Your wife is waiting for you and I don't want to keep you."

Stefan stood and nodded. He offered his hand. "Good night," he said and left the room.

Benjamin was immediately led out of the palace to the waiting car. He suspected that Mr. Bernard would have liked to dump him on the curb once they reached the villa, but the man exited the car and held the door open. "'Night, Bernard," Benjamin said.

"Good night, sir," the man said.

Benjamin walked to the front door and found Coco where he'd left her. No sounds coming from the nursery monitor. All was good. He picked up Coco and carried her to the bedroom where she'd slept last night. His hands itched to carry her soft body to his bed, but he knew better.

He just hoped tomorrow would be better for her than today had been. He slid her down to the bed and pulled the covers over her. She wiggled as if she were on the edge of awakening. Then she sighed and pressed her face into the pillow.

He should have resisted, but he didn't. Benjamin leaned down and brushed her cheek with his lips. She was the softest, sweetest thing he'd ever felt against his mouth.

"God help us. *Another family meeting,*" Bridget said to her sister, Phillipa, affectionately known as Pippa as they walked down the palace hallway toward Stefan's office. "Do you think he found out that we smiled at Coco Jordan? I'm starting to wonder if he used a hidden camera in the room while we were having tea."

"That would explain why he scowled at us just before he left yesterday," Pippa said. "It's ridiculous that he insists that we can't be friendly with her."

"I know," Bridget said. "I felt like I was kicking a puppy. She seemed very nice. I have a hard time believing her goal is to bring down the House of Devereaux."

"Someone has got to get through to Stefan," Pippa said.

"Good luck," Bridget said with a sigh. "The only one who can reason with him when he's like this is Eve, and she's having so much nausea from her pregnancy right now, I can't bring myself to bother her."

"I know," Pippa said, placing her hand over her own pregnant belly. "I had a few bad weeks, but it seems to have passed. Eve's just seems to be getting worse. Stefan's terribly worried about her, and I can't say I blame him."

"Well, here we go," Bridget said and knocked on Stefan's office door. The door immediately swung open and she was surprised to see Eve sitting in the room, eating a piece of toast. Stefan was on the phone.

"Eve, how wonderful to see you. How are you feeling?"

"Fine," Eve said, clearly fibbing. "I'm just not used to being restrained from regular activities. Plus, according to all the books, the nausea is supposed to have passed."

"I'm so sorry," Pippa said, hugging her sister-in-law.

"I am, too," Bridget said, reaching down to brush a kiss over her sister-in-law's cheek.

"How's the ranch coming?" Eve asked.

Bridget smiled at the fact that Stefan's wife hadn't forgotten the outrageous project Bridget and her Texas-born husband were pursuing. A ranch on Chantaine. "Thank you for asking. As you know, we're in the house. The whole ranch and animal thing will take a while."

"I'll help when I stop feeling so terrible," Eve said.

"Concentrate on taking care of yourself," Bridget said.

Eve made a face. "So boring." She glanced at Stefan, who was still on the phone. "So what did you think of Coco? Is she a villain in disguise?"

"I'd be shocked," Pippa said. "She was refreshingly genuine. I think you would have loved her. She says she loves to go fishing in her spare time, although she rarely has any spare time since she's taking care of a motherless baby. These are all clearly signs of a sociopath." Pippa scowled at her brother, who was too busy on his phone call to be aware of her.

"She did seem quite nice," Bridget said.

"What did Fredericka think?" Eve asked.

"Fredericka has more experience masking her emotions," Bridget said. "She's already gone back to Paris."

Eve's face fell. "What a shame. I would have liked her to meet Coco in better circumstances. That's why you're here. I insisted that Stefan allow you to meet Coco in a more natural, welcoming way. Her fiancé was ready to take her back to Texas. I think if dueling were still in style, he would have challenged Stefan."

Bridget gaped at Eve. "Engaged? I didn't know she was engaged."

"Apparently, she and her employer fell for each other. Easy to understand with the devotion she's showing to his daughter," Eve said.

"Hmm," Pippa said. "She didn't mention an engagement."

"We didn't exactly invite her to overshare, especially after Stefan showed up and gave us his devil glare," Bridget said.

"True," Pippa said and leaned toward Eve. "So what's the plan now?"

"We're going to have a family gathering today," Eve said. "With everyone. All the children."

"The twins?" Bridget echoed. Her beloved stepsons were sweet, but terribly active toddlers.

"Everyone. Even Stephenia," Eve said. "And we're inviting Coco and her fiancé and his baby. I believe her name is—"

"Emma," Pippa said. "I read the dossier," she added.

"Are husbands required to attend?" Bridget asked.

"It's not expected, at such short notice, but if you can coerce them, that would be wonderful," Eve said and munched on her toast.

"I'll try to tear Nic away from his satellite meetings," Pippa said doubtfully. "If he knows there's a time limit, I'm more likely to be successful."

"Ditto," Bridget said, thinking of her doctor husband's demanding schedule.

Stefan hung up his phone and turned to the group. "I have an announcement. We're going to have a family gathering this afternoon with Coco Jordan, her fiancé and his daughter."

"We already know," Bridget said. "We just need to know the start time."

Stefan frowned. "How would you know?"

"Did you really think we were going to sit here quietly while you talked on the phone?" Bridget asked.

Stefan narrowed his eyes. "There's no need to be disrespectful."

"There's no need to keep us waiting, Your Highness," she said, giving in to the need to needle her brother. She was the one most likely to push back besides Eve.

"Darling," Eve said, scrubbing her arm with a brush. "You were busy, so we already discussed the plans."

Stefan, clearly distracted by the way she scrubbed her arm, switched focus. "You're not feeling well, are you?"

"I'm fine," she said for the umpteenth time. "Your heir just likes sitting on my liver. Which makes me itch. It will end in a few months."

Stefan went to her side and cupped her cheek. "How can I make this up to you?"

"I'll think of something," Eve said and rubbed herself with the brush again.

After lunch, Coco, Benjamin and Emma entered the office of a palace advisor, George Singleton. "Welcome," he said, waving his hand to the two seats across from the desk. "It's my privilege to inform you of your inheritance from Prince Edward."

"Inheritance?" Coco echoed as she balanced Emma on her knee. She glanced at Benjamin in surprise.

"Just let Mr. Singleton bring you up to speed," he said.

She nodded. "Okay. Thank you, Mr. Singleton."

"Unfortunately, the prince's trust is set up to benefit the heirs who work for the benefit of the Devereaux. There is also a housing credit for all heirs who live on the palace grounds."

Coco nodded, but was having trouble taking it all in. Truth be told, she hadn't thought she'd inherit one penny from Prince Edward, since she was in her twenties when her paternity was revealed.

"Therefore you are due $103 American dollars per month after all taxes are removed. Additionally, you will receive an education stipend of $5,000 American dollars payable after your completion of an undergraduate degree."

"Oh," she murmured. "I couldn't finish my degree because my mother died."

Mr. Singleton cleared his throat. "Perhaps an exception could be made."

"Perhaps it could," Benjamin said.

Mr. Singleton nodded. "I'll discuss this with the other advisors. I must inform you that although it appears that royals lead an easy financial life, they must meet several criteria for financial support. The list of appearances they make is endless."

Coco nodded again. "I—"

Benjamin placed his hand over hers. "That doesn't alter any obligations toward Prince Edward's offspring—Coco."

Mr. Singleton sighed. "Very true, sir. I'll tell you the results of my discussion with the other royal advisors. Mr. Bernard shall now guide you to the family gathering. I understand you'll be meeting outside due to the favorable weather."

Mr. Singleton rose and extended his hand. "Miss Jordan," he said extending his hand. He turned to Benjamin. "Mr. Garner."

Benjamin shook the man's hand. "Nice meeting you."

"Thank you, sir," he said and Mr. Bernard arrived to lead them outside.

"It's a beautiful day. Princess Eve has determined that everyone would enjoy the warm sunshine. There will be a time at the playground so the children can release their energy. Princess Bridget's twins will especially enjoy the opportunity to play and explore, as will Princess Stephenia."

"Princess Stephenia?" Coco asked, trying to recall what she'd heard about the name.

"Princess Stephenia is Prince Stefan's daughter." He chuckled.

"Why do you laugh?" Coco asked.

Mr. Bernard frowned. "I'm not laughing."

"Yes, you did," Coco said. She sighed. "You're safe. We won't rat on you. Why did you laugh?"

Mr. Bernard slid her a sideways glance. "Princess Stephenia is quite the handful. When she arrived here, she screamed every time she encountered the prince."

"When she arrived?" Coco echoed.

Mr. Bernard pursed his lips. "That's all I have to say. Princess Stephenia is a delightful child."

Coco glanced at Benjamin. "Looks like you and Stefan may have more in common than you thought."

Benjamin glared at her.

The car stopped beside a playground with a slide, swings and climbing equipment. "It looks like a lot of fun for the children," Coco said.

"We are happy to please," Mr. Bernard said and moved outside the car to open the door. "A stroller will be brought to you for your convenience."

Surprised at the thoughtfulness, Coco automatically extended her hand to Mr. Bernard's arm. "Thank you. That is so very thoughtful."

Mr. Bernard looked at her in surprise then glanced away. "As I said, we're very happy to please. Call me for any need," he said and got back in the car.

She and Benjamin watched the car drive away.

"Weird guy," Benjamin said.

"But nice," she said. "I think the royal stuff keeps him from being too real."

Benjamin shrugged. "Maybe. Let's give Emma a try in the swing before everyone else shows up."

Coco smiled. "Great idea."

They strapped Emma into the baby swing and Benjamin gently pushed it from the front. Coco stood to the side and watched the baby's eyes grow round. Benjamin increased the force of the push and Emma began to laugh. With each successive swing, she let out a shriek of delight.

Seeing Benjamin with his baby girl in such a happy moment brought tears to Coco's eyes. When she'd first arrived at Benjamin's home, they'd both seemed terrified of each other. Now they were truly starting to bond. Coco knew that Emma was one lucky girl. Benjamin was on the road to becoming a terrific father. She was so caught up in watching Benjamin and Emma that she didn't notice Princess Phillipa until she appeared by her side.

"Oh, hello, Your Highness," Coco said and started to curtsey.

Phillipa shook her head. "Not necessary, and please call me Pippa." She pointed toward Benjamin and Emma on the swings. "He looks like excellent husband material. I hear congratulations are in order for your engagement."

Coco blinked for a few seconds then remembered the pretend agreement she and Benjamin had made. "Thank you," she said, uneasy with the deception. "It was nice of Prince Stefan to arrange this time on the playground for us."

Pippa chuckled. "You can thank Eve for that. Ah, here she comes, along with Stephenia, and the twins and Bridget bringing up the rear. When will Bridget learn not to wear heels when she's chasing toddlers?"

"Boys, Stephenia," Pippa said, stepping in front of the galloping toddlers. "Careful of the swing."

The three youngsters stared at the baby in the swing. The little girl with ringlet curls pointed at Emma. "Who?"

"That's Emma," Pippa said. "She belongs to Mr. Garner and Miss Jordan."

Benjamin waved at the kids and Pippa made the introductions. He continued to push Emma in the swing. The toddlers scrambled onto the various pieces of miniature playground equipment.

"I didn't realize there were so many children," Coco said, trying to recall what she'd read about the Devereaux offspring on the internet.

"And more on the way," Pippa said, touching her abdomen. "Eve is due before I am, but I'm having such an easy time compared to her that I feel guilty."

"Oh, I'm sorry to hear that," Coco said to the tall, dark-haired woman.

"It's not high-risk, just extremely uncomfortable," Eve said.

"How are you feeling today?" Pippa asked Eve.

"I'm fine. I slept longer than usual," Eve said then turned to Coco. "Coco, it's my pleasure to meet you and welcome you to where the wild things grow here in Chantaine," she said with a smile. "I hope you'll enjoy your time here."

Bridget glanced around the playground. "Where are my little darlings?" she muttered, narrowing her eyes. "Ah, in the hide-and-seek house. Should have known." She turned to Coco and smiled. "So nice to see you again. That's a darling baby in the swing. Hope the man is just as darling, too. The Devereaux seem to have a weakness for Texans."

A shriek of distress sounded from the other side of the hide-and-seek house. "Excuse me," Bridget said. "That's mine. I know his voice."

"I never would have believed what a great mother she's become," Pippa said.

"She fell for the doctor and his boys hook, line and sinker," Eve said. "A joy to watch. Bridget always gave the impression of being the royal fashion plate, and single forever. Turns out her heart was squishier than she thought."

At that moment, Coco began to feel a little hope that maybe she wasn't completely alone in the world after all. Maybe the Devereaux actually were a little bit like her. At least on the inside.

After playtime, which included Benjamin chasing the toddlers and making them laugh until they were breathless, everyone went inside for lunch. Nannies arrived to take the children when they grew restless. Stephenia, however, wanted to stay, and Eve permitted it.

Coco noticed that Benjamin talked very little. She could practically feel his mind clicking with all his observations. He put his hand over hers and her brain instantly stuttered. Even though she knew his touch was just for show, it still affected her. Bridget gave her apologies as she left for an event at a library. Pippa received a call from her husband and left the room to take it.

Eve had seemed to grow much more weary as the day proceeded. Coco feared that Eve's desire to make her feel welcome was making Eve stay longer than she should. "It's been wonderful having this opportunity to get to know all of you better. I can't tell you how much I've appreciated the time with you. We should probably get back so Emma can take a nap."

"Are you sure I can't do anything else for you?" Eve asked as she shared a small cookie with Stephenia while the toddler sat on her lap.

"Not a thing," Coco said and stood.

"Well, if you're sure," she said and set Stephenia on her feet. Eve stood, and the blood appeared to drain from her face. "Oh," she murmured and collapsed onto the floor.

Benjamin was by the woman's side in an instant. Stephenia began to cry, so Coco set Emma on a blanket and picked up the distressed toddler. "Is she okay?" Coco asked. "We need to get help," she said and stepped into the hallway where a man stood outside the door.

Moments later, the room was filled with a doctor, nurse, two guards and Pippa.

"I keep telling her she's doing too much, but she won't listen," Pippa said, wringing her hands. "She's just not used to sitting still for anything. She thinks it's a sign of weakness."

"True Texan spirit," Benjamin said, now holding Emma. "Good luck to her husband."

Stephenia was still upset, but quiet as she clung to

Coco with one hand and soothed herself with her thumb in her mouth. "She'll be okay," Coco said to the child resting on her hip. "See, she's sitting up."

"Already fussing at the doctor," Pippa said in a wry tone.

Eve waved aside the crowd around her and stood. The doctor and guards, however, stayed within arm's reach. "I'm fine. Completely fine."

"One of the top lies spoken every day," Benjamin said in a low voice.

Eve glanced across the room and spotted them. "Oh, no. I've frightened Stephenia," she said, walking toward Coco.

"She's okay," Coco said and set the toddler down onto her feet.

"Mamaeve," Stephenia wailed, lifting her arms for a hug.

Eve bent down and Benjamin pulled out a chair for her to sit down. Eve flashed a look of impatience. "Honestly, there's no need for a fuss."

"The fainting thing cancels out your denial. You know the old saying—actions speak louder than words," Benjamin said.

"I'm glad someone else said that," Pippa said.

Eve still looked irritated. "I don't like being forced to sit."

"You're not being forced," Coco said. "You're being helped."

Eve rolled her eyes in disbelief.

"It's true," Coco said. "You have a very important job to do. Probably one of the most important jobs of your life. You're nurturing a baby. There are two lives at stake and both are very important to many people. Even though it seems that sitting down or resting is being lazy, it's not. You probably think it's difficult and boring, but it's a necessary part of your job."

Eve stared at Coco for a long moment. "I guess I never thought of it that way. I just expected to take pregnancy in stride and keep doing what I've always done." She glanced at her doctor. "I guess it doesn't always work out that way."

"Quite true, Your Highness," he said.

"I'm just not the fainting type," Eve said.

"As long as you follow the doctor's direction, you won't become the fainting type," Pippa said. "Like you were today."

Eve bared her teeth slightly then sighed. "Okay, my job is to gestate. Hopefully someone will help amuse me."

"The line forms behind me," Pippa said with a smile.

Coco felt another invisible thread connecting her to Eve and Pippa.

That evening after Coco and Benjamin both bathed Emma, they sat on the love seat and propped their feet on pillows placed on the coffee table. Benjamin rotated between a soccer game and a television show on the BBC.

"I feel like I need subtitles. The British English is so different from Texas English," Benjamin said.

Coco laughed, and the sound made his chest tighten and expand.

"Does that mean you feel the same way?" he asked.

"I guess so. I just never thought of it that way," she said and met his gaze. "Thanks for being with me today. Between the meeting with the advisor and Eve fainting, it was a roller-coaster ride."

He nodded. "Yeah. What do you think of the Devereaux now?"

"I think they bleed," she said. "Like you and me."

He met her gaze and something inside him grew and expanded. Coco was deep, sometimes sad, but he could tell that she kept trying to be positive and hopeful. Despite everything she'd been through, she wanted to give people the benefit of the doubt. Being with her made him want to be less cynical.

"You did well today," he said.

She laced her fingers together then unlaced them. He covered her hand and her fidgeting stopped. She glanced up to meet his gaze. The moment stretched between them.

Fighting a massive internal debate, Benjamin lowered his mouth to hers. Slowly. Slowly enough that she could turn away if she wanted. But she didn't. Her gaze was locked with his. Her eyelids lowered with each millimeter he drew closer. He wanted to take her mouth, absorb her into him. He wanted to rush, but he made himself go slow.

Eons seemed to pass. He finally pressed his mouth against hers. Her lips were soft and sweet. There was a sense of waiting and wanting in the air. He inhaled briefly, wanting to focus on her mouth.

She responded, rubbing her lips against his.

The sensation of need ran through him like wildfire, and he felt a little of his self-control shatter. Clenching his hand into a fist, he tried to regain control. But then she rubbed her lips against him again and he felt it all the way down from his mouth to his chest to his gut to his groin.

Benjamin opened his mouth and slid his tongue into her mouth. She tasted sweet and wild. When she slipped her hands around his neck, he just wanted more.

Chapter Eight

Coco felt as if she were stuck on the top of a ferris wheel. She sank against Benjamin's chest as his mouth took hers. She hadn't allowed herself to want him. She'd scolded herself not to be attracted to him. He was her boss, and he was wounded from his experience with Emma's mother. A bad combination.

But now he felt strong and everything about him was too seductive to resist. The way he kissed her, the way he held her. He deepened the kiss further and her breath seemed to stop in her throat. She felt a terrible restlessness that invaded her from head to toe, with special emphasis in between. She wriggled against him to soothe the sensation, but that just seemed to make it worse.

Benjamin let out a low groan and the sound vibrated

inside her. Leaning backward, he dragged her on top of him. One of his hands slid to cup her breast while his other pressed her pelvis against him. His unmistakable hardness found the place between her legs where she began to ache.

She tugged at his shirt, wanting to feel his bare skin. He growled in approval and seconds later she felt her naked breasts against his chest. With her skirt and his jeans between them, she just wanted to get rid of everything keeping her from being as close as possible to him.

He must have heard her need. Benjamin found the zipper to her skirt and pushed it down, along with her panties. Finally, she was naked. All she needed was to help him get rid of his jeans and underwear and—

A muffled sound emanated from the baby monitor. Coco was so turned on she wasn't sure that she'd heard correctly. Benjamin continued to caress and kiss her, making her hotter with each passing stroke.

Another sound from the baby monitor. This one louder. Another that turned into a wail. Coco stilled as her heartbeat throbbed in her ears and throughout every pulse point in the body. Benjamin didn't seem to hear.

"It's Emma," she finally managed to say. "She's awake. And crying."

Benjamin pulled his mouth away from hers, his eyes dark with the same need she felt. When Emma let out another cry, realization crossed his face. He swore under his breath and helped both her and himself into a sitting position.

Coco was still aroused, but she suddenly felt self-conscious by the contrast of her complete nudity and Benjamin's half-dressed state. Fumbling with her blouse, she struggled to find the buttons. "I'll get her," she said. "I just need to put on my clothes."

"No, it's okay," he said as he stood. "I'll do it." He pulled on his shirt and left the room.

The blouse was turned half-inside-out, making the act of dressing herself that much more frustrating. She finally put it on, then pulled on her panties and skirt. When she stood, she suspected her panties were on backward.

Confused about what she should do next, she pushed her hair out of her face and walked toward the room where Emma was supposed to be sleeping. She glanced inside in the darkness and saw the outline of Benjamin standing as he rocked from side to side with Emma in his arms.

She didn't want to interrupt because it appeared he'd successfully quieted her. Her heart twisted. More progress between Dad and his daughter. A few moments ago, however, she'd thought of him as anything but a dad.

Coco stood there for a few moments to collect her breath and sense. What did it mean that they had nearly made love? What next? Should she stay awake or try to go to sleep?

Slowly, she walked to her bedroom and sank onto the bed, her head still spinning. Coco could hardly believe that Benjamin was really interested in *her*. She'd always viewed herself as very ordinary, but with determination. That determination had kept her sane during life's less sane moments. And this was one crazy moment. Coco knew that she was no bombshell, like the woman who had given birth to Benjamin's child.

Wash your face. Brush your teeth. Things will be clearer in the morning. How many times had her mother repeated those words to her? Coco followed her mother's advice, then crawled into bed and told herself to stop thinking about Benjamin. But then she turned on the baby monitor just in case Benjamin went to sleep and Emma awakened again.

In a low voice, more breath than song, Benjamin hummed a lullaby to Emma. Her heart swelled so much it hurt at the loving sound, and she closed her eyes at her odd instinct to cry. She was no crybaby. Why was this happening to her? She couldn't remember a man affecting her so deeply. It was as if he reached her on a cellular level. The possibility was disturbing. She took a deep breath to still the feelings rolling through her.

She tried counting backward from one hundred to fall asleep, but somehow Benjamin's lullaby made her drift off.

The next morning she awakened to the sound of Emma chattering through the nursery monitor. She allowed the baby to experience some time by herself. It was good for Emma to self-soothe for a short time.

Coco's mind wandered to thoughts about Benjamin. Something inside her had solidified. She knew she had strong feelings for him. She knew he was important to her. Coco smiled and bounced out of bed, ready for the day. Ready for her future with whatever happened between her and Benjamin.

She threw on some clothes and made a quick trip to wash her face and brush her teeth then raced into Emma's room. "Well, good mornin' darlin'," she said as the baby began to fuss.

Emma glanced at her and gave a welcoming chortle.

Coco changed the baby and picked her up. "Who wants a bottle and breakfast?"

Emma began her version of a morning chat with unintelligible, but happy sounds. "Bottle first?" A moment later, Coco warmed a bottle and sat on the sofa to feed the baby. Emma gave a few burps and Coco put her in the pack and play.

Coco grabbed a quick shower. When she walked out of her bedroom dressed, with wet hair, Benjamin greeted her in the hallway. "'Morning," he said.

Her heart hammered against her chest. "'Morning," she returned. "I've already given Emma her bottle. She should be ready for breakfast soon. Did she keep you awake too long last night?"

"Just awhile," he said, and raked his hand through his damp hair. "Listen, I'm sorry about last night. That shouldn't have happened. I shouldn't have—" He broke off.

Her heart felt as if it broke in half. "Shouldn't have?" she prompted.

"Shouldn't have kissed you. Shouldn't have gone after you like that," he said.

She worked hard to take a breath. "Are you saying you didn't want me?" she managed, confused and so hurt.

"Not want you," he echoed and looked away. "At that moment, I did," he said. "But it still shouldn't have happened. I don't want you to start thinking this engagement is real. Last night wouldn't have happened if we were still in Texas." He met her gaze. "I can't get into a relationship right now. I have too much going on."

Coco crossed her arms over her chest. "Is that the same way you felt about Brooke?"

He took a sharp breath and shook his head. "Brooke was a crazy impulse. I broke all my rules. I don't want to do that again."

She struggled to swallow over the lump in her throat. "Okay. I'll feed Emma."

She turned away and felt his hand on her arm. But she didn't turn to look at him because she wasn't sure she could control her facial expression. "I don't want to hurt you. That's why we can't do this."

She pulled her arm away from him. "I'll feed Emma."

Thank goodness for the baby. She demanded and received so much of Coco's attention that for the next several hours, she managed not to look Benjamin in the eye. It was for the best. What should have been a make-out session had turned into something far more for Coco. Crazy. Stupid. She would be more careful from this moment on. She wouldn't give in to silly secret feelings for Benjamin. She just wished she'd never given herself permission to even consider Benjamin as *her man.*

After spending most of the day inside, Coco was ready to scream. She needed to get out. She needed to get away from Benjamin. She called Mr. Bernard to ask about an outing. He suggested a few possibilities and Coco selected the beach. Slathering Emma with baby-safe sunscreen and dressing her in a protective baby bathing suit, Coco plopped a hat on the tot's head and got ready.

When Mr. Bernard knocked at the door, Coco was just about ready.

Benjamin answered the door and Coco grabbed Emma and raced to greet their guide. "Emma and I are going to the beach," she said breathlessly. "We'll see you later," she said and walked out the door, feeling a smidgeon of self-satisfaction that Benjamin was staring after her and the baby with a surprised look on his face.

Mr. Bernard told her a bit about Chantaine's beaches and warned her that the ocean temperature might be a little chilly for the baby. She appreciated his consideration. With help from him, she was quickly situated on the beach with an umbrella, chaise longue and an extra-large towel.

Coco put Emma in her infant carrier, and for once, the baby didn't struggle to escape. Emma sat, appearing relaxed, with her eyes half-open. Coco smiled at the sight of Emma, wondering if the sound of the ocean was soothing to the baby.

Sighing, she leaned back against her chair and let the breeze and surf sounds assuage her own riot of feelings and thoughts. With one eye on Emma, Coco watched the soft whitecaps as they gently met the shore. She wondered how often Prince Edward had taken solace at the sight of the sea. Everyone had told her how much he had loved yachting.

The last time Coco had been to the ocean had been three years ago—a too-brief trip with college friends. Her favorite part of that trip had been a walk on the beach by herself. Was that something she had in common with her birth father? Or was it just crazy to consider that she had anything in common with him except some genetic material?

Coco dismissed her debates and focused on the peace and relaxation of the moment. Emma was quietly content, the sun was shining, and Benjamin wasn't nearby to disrupt her—although his presence wasn't required to mess with her mind. Just a thought would do.

"Hello, hello," a voice called from behind her.

Coco glanced up to see Bridget walking toward her, wearing a bright pink hat, a pink suit and pink heels. In the sand? Coco stood and watched as a man followed after the princess carrying a chair. "Thanks so much, Anthony. I won't be long," she said to the man then turned to Coco. "Would you like a little cocktail?"

"I'm good with my water," Coco said. "What a surprise."

Bridget shot a sly look and sank onto the chair. "I'm good with those," she said. "I hope I'm not interrupting, but I heard you were having some beach time and since I was driving by, I thought it might be fun to make a little stop." She glanced down at Emma, who was regarding the princess with curiosity. "Do we have a little beach baby here?"

"I think this is her first ocean sighting and she seems to love it. The sound of the waves and the breeze. It affects me that way," Coco said. "It was nice of you to stop by."

"My pleasure. I'm in between appearances today. I'll turn into ranch frau tomorrow. The things I do to please my husband," she said, making a tsk-ing sound. "Well, he did give up his career in Dallas to move to my country and my brother immediately saddled him with a hugely challenging job. I would do anything for him, even though he drives me crazy," Bridget said. "I'm sure it the same with you and your Benjamin."

Coco clenched her teeth for a moment then produced a smile. "I wonder if all men make their women crazy."

"Oh, they must," Bridget said. "You've probably heard that whole Venus and Mars thing. Well, scientists have conducted a study on the differences between men and women, and they say we're so different we could be different species. Pippa the brainiac told me that. So now scientists are telling us what we've always known. Men are aliens."

Coco laughed despite the fact that her heart was still hurting. "And you have two little males, too," Coco said.

"I know. And I love all three of my men. The twins are always doing something that makes me laugh and sometimes cry. I suspect the same thing has happened with you and little Emma," Bridget said, glancing at the baby. "Oh, look, she's blowing bubbles. I miss those days."

"If you miss it that much, you could have a baby," Coco drawled.

"*Mon dieu,* no," Bridget said. "I'm sure I'll do it one day, but Ryder, the boys and this *ranch* keep me quite busy enough." She shot Coco a sideways smile. "Cheeky of you to suggest it, though. Sounds like something I might say to one of my sisters."

A throwaway comment, but the word *sisters* caught at Coco's heart.

"Well, enough about that subject," Bridget said. "The other reason I wanted to chat with you is because there's going to be a charity gala at the palace in a few days. And we would like you to join us."

Surprise raced through Coco. "Charity gala," she echoed and shook her head. "That's so nice of you, but I would need a babysitter. And I can't imagine I have anything to wear. And—"

"Excuses, excuses," Bridget said. "We have several wonderful nannies who would provide excellent care for

Emma. And although no one would accuse us of having runway fashions to rival Paris, we do have a few nice boutiques."

Coco could easily imagine that the price of a dress in one of those boutiques would require at least a month of her pay. "Oh, I don't know," she said, thinking the event sounded like the adult version of prom.

"Eve, Pippa and I will be very sad if you don't attend," Bridget said.

"And Stefan?" Coco asked, although she suspected she already knew the answer. Stefan would love for her to just disappear.

"Stefan is secretly grateful to you for telling Eve that she is doing a job by being pregnant. No one has been able to get her to slow down. *Slow down* and *Eve* don't belong in the same sentence. She's one of those save-the-world types," Bridget said.

"Like you?" Coco asked and took a sip of water.

Bridget twitched her lips. "There you go being cheeky again. We can go shopping for your dress tomorrow," Bridget said and rose to her feet. She waved for her chauffeur. "Time for me to go. Thanks for letting me join—"

Panic set in. "Bridget, I'm very honored by your invitation, but I don't think—"

"I don't want you to be honored. I want you to attend," Bridget said. "Don't tell me you don't like shopping. I had that trouble with Eve and Pippa," she said, shaking her head.

"That's it," Coco fibbed. "I'm just not much of a shopper."

"Well, I'll just have to pick something out for you and send it over. Will Benjamin need a suit?" Bridget asked.

"No, but—"

"But nothing. If he brought a suit, he's ready."

"I'm not sure this is his kind of party," Coco said.

"It won't be that bad. There will be beer available and Benjamin can chat with Ryder about sports. He misses that." She brushed her hands together. "There. All done. I'll talk to you soon. Ciao, darling."

A couple hours later, Coco strolled into the villa toting Emma.

"How was your time at the beach?" Benjamin asked.

"Great," Coco said. "I found out we're going to a charity gala sometime soon."

"What?" he said.

She felt a quick tension in her belly, but pushed it aside. "No problem. You have a suit, so you should be good. Plus, they'll serve beer, and Bridget's doctor husband is from Texas and he'll want to talk sports."

"What about Emma?" he asked.

"They have nannies galore," she said and foisted Emma into his arms. "I need a shower."

Coco headed straight for the bathroom, turned on the shower and hopped inside. She enjoyed the warm spray over her head and body and willed the water to wash away her worries.

* * *

Benjamin changed his daughter's diaper and gave her a bottle. He wondered if he should bathe her. He wondered when the hell Coco was going to come see him. He pulled some baby food from the counter, plunked Emma into her infant seat, and began to spoon some green substance into his daughter's mouth.

"Airplane flying through the sky," he said, feeding Emma.

"Nice technique," Coco said, walking into the room. She wore a white robe far larger than she was.

"I have to get creative," Benjamin said and sailed another foot into Emma's mouth. "Wanna take over?" he asked.

"But you're doing so well," she said.

Benjamin sighed.

Emma gave a raspberry, sending her green food all over Benjamin's chest.

"I think she's done with dinner," Coco said.

Benjamin shot Coco a dark look. "Ya think?"

Emma gave another raspberry and he would have sworn he heard Coco snicker, but he was too busy protecting himself from some vile puréed vegetable to check. He rubbed Emma with a cloth and she began to fuss.

"I'll take her then I'll go to bed," Coco said.

"TV is out here," he pointed out.

"I can read a book. G'night," she said.

"But—" Benjamin said as Coco lifted Emma from the baby seat.

"We're good," Coco said and took Benjamin's daughter to the bathroom.

"You sure I can't help?" he asked.

"No. We're taking a bath," Coco said.

Benjamin visualized Coco taking a bath and his body instantly tightened. He walked toward the bathroom and spied Emma in the bathtub. She gurgled at Coco, who encouraged her.

He paused before speaking. "Does she like this?"

"In the right conditions," Coco said. "Optimal temperature, etc…"

"How do you know all this?" he asked.

"Experiment and practice," Coco said, still not looking at him, which irritated him.

"You wanna give me a clue?" he asked.

"Soon enough," she said. "I'll write it all down, but there are a lot of particulars."

"Is that a woman thing?" he asked.

Coco rinsed Emma and pulled her from the tub. She shot him a sideways glance. "There are particulars for every baby. Male or female."

"But in my baby's case?"

"She likes berry-scented soap and her fave temp is almost hot. She loves a sip of apple juice while she's in the tub…"

"Hell, that sounds like an apple-tini," Benjamin said.

"No vodka needed for Miss Emma," she said. "Just good hugs and a lullaby."

"And what about the nanny?"

Coco paused for a long moment and bit her lip. "Not your problem."

"Why do I feel like it is?" he asked.

"Misplaced responsibility?" she asked and placed Emma in his arms. "Enjoy your sweetie pie. I'm going to bed."

"Whoa," Benjamin said. "She looks like she'll be gone for the night in just a few minutes. Flat-screen is available as soon as she's asleep."

"I need to protect myself," Coco said.

"What do you mean?" he asked.

"I mean that you are dangerous at night. I need to avoid you then," she said and turned away.

Benjamin held his daughter as he watched Coco walk away, and he suddenly felt alone. Regret filled him, tightening his chest and spreading outward.

"Hey," he said. "Are you sure you're okay?"

She glanced over her shoulder, but didn't meet his eyes. "I'm great. Let me know if you need help with Emma."

"I will," he said, feeling alone. Very alone. He knew he had made a mistake kissing Coco and undressing her as he had. On the other hand, he hadn't slept last night, either, and he'd thought about her all day.

Maybe another night would cure him, he hoped. If

not, another day would do it. He swore under his breath. If twenty-four hours didn't do it, then he would need help.

A couple hours later, Benjamin went to bed. It took a while for him to fall asleep. A vision swam before him. Coco appeared and lowered her mouth to his. Time passed in a millisecond and she was naked against him. He realized that he was also naked and her breasts felt delicious against his bare chest. Her nipples were taut and sensitive as he touched them.

Her moan made him unbearably aroused. *I want you,* he said.

I want you, she echoed.

Seconds later, he slid his hand between them to the top of her thighs where she was moist and swollen. He stroked her as he kissed her.

"You feel so good," he said, sinking into her kiss and the intimate sensation of being so close to her. His breath hitched in his throat and he stretched toward her, wanting to be inside her.

Finally, he thrust inside, where she was wet and warm. He pumped, feeling the sweat bead on his forehead. His heart hammered against his chest. He was so aroused he could explode.

Coco stretched her legs around him and held him close. "I love you," she whispered.

Her words stopped his heart. "Don't love me," he said. "I'm not the right man for you. Not right now."

"I love you anyway," she said.

He felt himself rise again inside her. Swearing, he couldn't hold himself back. Even though she'd told him she'd loved him. Even though she shouldn't love him, and he shouldn't let her.

But he couldn't control the way she made love to him with her body, and he couldn't stop the way he made love to her with his body, either. He began again the rhythm of sinking himself inside her. He felt himself grow closer and closer to release. He was almost there....

He woke up, sweating, his pulse racing, and he was as hard as a brick. It took him a few seconds to separate the dream from reality. Coco was not in his bed whispering alarming words in his ear while they made love to each other.

"Thank God," he muttered as he sat up, though his body was in complete disagreement. His body clamored for satisfaction, and his heart— His heart wasn't involved, he told himself. His heart had no room for the woman who was the nanny to his daughter and who had just learned she was part royal.

The next morning, Coco tried to avoid Benjamin, which was difficult because the villa wasn't that large. So she took Emma for walks in the stroller. Three of them. She was just about to leave for a walk on her own when Bridget called.

"Time for shopping," Bridget said. "Now don't turn

me down. I know you're not doing anything. Mr. Bernard reports that you've taken Emma on multiple walks."

"I don't know, Bridget," she said and decided to be honest. "These boutiques may be a bit out of my price range."

"Oh, don't worry about that. Eve wants to give this to you as a gift," Bridget said.

"Oh, no. I couldn't," she said, horrified at the prospect.

"She'll be terribly offended if you don't accept. Eve is so kind and wonderful. You wouldn't want to offend her, would you?" Bridget asked, and Coco couldn't help thinking she was being played.

"I'm sure she would get over it," Coco drawled.

"Oh, stop being so difficult. Even if you don't find anything you like, it will get you off the palace grounds, and you shouldn't miss Chantaine's downtown area. Some find it quite quaint."

Coco couldn't disagree with the idea of escaping Benjamin for a while. "All right," she said. "You're very kind to invite me, but don't count on coming back with anything for me."

Soon enough, Coco learned that Bridget was one pushy princess. "Oh, please," Bridget said after they'd cruised through the second boutique. "You're making this miserable. There's got to be something you like. There are so many dresses that would look wonderful on you."

Coco shrugged. All the prices had been out of her

range so far. "You know how it is when you can't find exactly the right dress," Coco said as she sifted through a rack of dresses. She wandered toward a sale rack in the back of the store.

"Trust me, there's nothing there," Bridget said. "Come back up front."

Coco continued to flip through the rack and found a simple sapphire-blue full-length dress. The price was still a little high, but…

Bridget came to her side. "Lovely color. A little plain, but with a little jewelry, it would do." She glanced at Coco and smiled. "You have Devereaux eyes, only a little sweeter."

"You're the sweet one," Coco said. "Putting up with me to do all this shopping."

"Oh, trust me," Bridget said. "This is a pleasure after playing ranch frau this morning. Now try on your plain dress. I'm ready to disapprove and we'll move on to the next shop."

Coco tried on the dress and loved it. She loved that the color was vibrant and the design simple, a V-neck with an A-line that flattered her slim frame.

Bridget crossed her arms over her chest and shook her head. "I want to veto it, but something about it is perfect. We can do something with your hair, give you some jewelry, the right shoes."

"Shoes?" Coco echoed. "I have black heels."

"We can do better than that," Bridget said.

Coco felt a sinking sensation. "Better than black heels?"

"Of course we can," Bridget said.

Coco wrestled with Bridget to pay the bill. For a moment there, it could have gotten bloody, but Coco pulled out the guilt screws. "This is embarrassing me," Coco said.

Bridget immediately backed off. For a full moment. "Fine," she said. "But I'm still getting your shoes."

Chapter Nine

Two nights later, Benjamin paced the front room, dressed in his suit, tugging at his shirt collar. What had possessed him to agree to go to this gala? He could have said no-how, no-way, but he'd thought his absence might look odd since he and Coco were supposed to be *engaged.*

Now he was stuck with what would likely be the most uncomfortable evening of his life. He took another gulp of water and paced the front room again.

Out of the corner of his eye, he spotted a vibrant blue color and he spun around. Coco entered the hallway, looking beautiful in a long evening gown with a sparkly headband and bracelet. Her hair was a mass of tousled waves, her face enhanced with a hint more makeup than usual. Her lips glistened and she licked them, making him wanting to kiss her.

"Do I look okay?" she asked.

He shook his head. "No. You look beautiful," he said.

Relief smoothed out her features. "Thanks. You didn't have to say that."

"It's true. That dress looks great on you. The color almost matches your eyes."

"Thanks. I found it on the sale rack."

"You didn't have to get a clearance dress," he said.

"I didn't want to overspend. And I didn't want the Devereaux to pay for it, even though Bridget insisted they would," she said and fiddled with her wrap.

"I would have bought you a dress. Heaven knows you're due a bonus after dealing with Emma nonstop," he said, chuckling.

She met his gaze and smiled. "Maybe, but I wanted to pay for this myself."

"You just didn't want to be one of those illegitimate moochers," he joked with her.

She laughed with him. "You've got that right. I know you can't wait to go tonight."

"Oh, I've been so excited all day that I can hardly stand it," he said in a dry tone. "I haven't been this excited since I went to the Super Bowl."

She swatted his chest. "Liar, liar, pants on fire," she said.

"Ouch, you have a mean right hook," he said.

"Again, liar, liar—"

He held up his hands, enjoying the fact that she was acting relaxed with him. Since the night they'd almost had sex, she'd frozen him out. He knew he deserved it, but it sure as hell didn't feel good.

"Okay, okay," he said. "When is the babysitter supposed to get here?" he asked.

As if on cue, a knock sounded at the door. Benjamin answered and a young woman entered.

"Please forgive me. I'm Natalie and I've been helping Princess Bridget's twins. I'm here to take care of your baby, Emma. Are there any specific instructions?" she asked.

"If the bottle doesn't work, you can give her a small amount of cereal," Coco said.

"She likes Cheerios, but hopefully she won't be awake long enough for that," Benjamin said. "If she wakes up after you've put her to bed, when all else fails, sing to her."

"But she loves to be rocked," Coco added.

And so it went for several moments. Natalie duly wrote down all of Benjamin and Coco's instructions and suggestions, which, after all was said and done, could have been the first chapter of a book.

"You'll call if you have any problems at all?" Coco asked, halfway wishing she could stay in the villa instead of going to the gala. She was growing more nervous with each passing moment.

"Enjoy the party," Natalie said. "Your baby will probably sleep all the way through. If she doesn't, I will rock her and sing to her."

Coco felt a surge of relief. "Thank you. But you'll call…"

"Yes, I will call. Please go and enjoy," Natalie said. "Your car is waiting."

Coco took a deep breath. "Then we should leave," she said and glanced at Benjamin.

"Yes, we should," he said and ushered her out of the villa to the car.

Benjamin looked amazing, Coco thought, as he helped her into the car. He was dressed Texan formal in a black suit, bolo tie and his black hat. He hadn't worn his hat in a while so he wouldn't frighten Emma. He looked sexy enough to kill. And it would take all she had not to be the victim of this murder.

She crossed her left leg over her right and pumped it.

"That's some shoe," Benjamin said.

Coco glanced down at the sparkly pump and smiled. "Yes, it is. Bridget insisted. I insisted that it was on sale, which it was." She pumped her foot again. "It almost looks like Cinderella's slipper, doesn't it?"

"Well, I never wore Cinderella's slipper, but yeah, I can see the resemblance," he said. "Nice legs."

Coco immediately pushed her dress over her leg. "Thank you," she murmured.

Seconds later, the limo stopped in front of the palace and the driver escorted them out of the car.

"Thank you," Benjamin said and slid his hand behind Coco's waist. "Nice that they let us in the front door this time," he said.

She glanced up at him and felt a camera flash, saw it in her peripheral vision. "This is going to be different," she managed, meeting his gaze.

"Get ready for the circus, darlin'," Benjamin said and they walked inside the palace.

A string orchestra played beautiful music and waiters served appetizers and champagne. The chandeliers sparkled like diamonds. The marble floors gleamed, making Coco fear she'd fall on her derriere! A girl needed tennis shoes, not heels, in this situation.

"It's so beautiful," Coco said. "Look at all the dresses."

"If you say so," Benjamin said. He nodded at a server. "Can you get me a beer?"

"Yes, sir. I'll be right back," the server said.

"Bet it won't take him long," Coco said.

"Why?" Benjamin asked.

"Because you're so threatening," Coco said.

"I'm not threatening," Benjamin protested. "I just want a beer."

Coco snickered. "You still scared him."

Benjamin shot her a mock frown. "Why aren't *you* more afraid of me?"

"Because I am magic for your daughter," she said.

Benjamin shrugged. "Can't deny that," he said and suddenly his beer appeared. He glanced at Coco and lifted an eyebrow before he nodded at the server. "Thanks."

"My pleasure, sir. Please let me know if you need anything else," the server said and walked away.

A man in uniform appeared at the top of the double staircase and rang a bell. "Please proceed to the ballroom to your right. The royal family will arrive soon."

The crowd moved toward the ballroom, and Coco became separated from Benjamin. She craned her neck to find him in the crowd, but couldn't see him. She should have been able to see him with his Stetson, but every time she looked above the crowd, someone raised an arm or a tall man walked in front of her.

"Lovely lady," a man said to her.

Coco glanced to her right and gazed at a middle-aged man with piercing blue eyes. "Thank you," she said. "Please excuse me..."

"A Yank," the man said in delight. "An American. We're deluged with Italians and French. How did this happen?"

Coco shrugged. "Lucky, I guess," she said.

A half beat later, she felt a tap on her shoulder and she turned around, hoping it was Benjamin. Instead, it was Bridget.

"How are your shoes?" Bridget asked with a beaming smile.

Coco paused then gave a mangled curtsey. "Your Highness," she said.

Bridget waved the courtesy aside. "Oh, stop. Show me your shoes."

Coco obediently lifted her Cinderella pumps. Bridget clapped her hands and smiled. "Excellent. You look ravishing. I'll check in with you later." She looked past Coco and her smile fell. "Oh, hello, Rodney. *Ciao*."

"You're good friends with the princess," Rodney said as Bridget walked away.

"No, not really," Coco said.

"You must be. She was quite friendly with you and knew about your shoes." Rodney squinted at her. "You have the Devereaux eyes," he exclaimed. "You have an American accent." His eyes widened in recognition. "I saw your photo on the internet. You're the illegitimate Devereaux. No wonder Princess Bridget was nice to you. I'm sure Stefan gave her instructions."

Dismayed, Coco stared at him.

"And I'm Rodney, your third or fourth cousin," he said, extending his hand. "I'm a black sheep of the family, too. You're safe with me," he said in a confidential tone.

But somehow she didn't feel so safe. Instead, Coco felt confused and uncomfortable. "I need to leave," she said.

"Stay with me. I can make introductions," Rodney said.

"Oh, no, that's okay," Coco said. "I need to find my date. A pleasure to meet you," she fibbed with a shrug and rushed away. Luckily enough, she ran far enough to run into Benjamin.

"Thank goodness," she said.

"Trouble?" he asked.

"Some distant cousin of the Devereaux started asking questions. I had a hard time getting away from him," she said.

"Then stay with me," he said and enclosed her arm inside hers. "No one is competing for my presence."

"Bet it's the hat or the bolo," she said, unable to keep herself from smiling.

"Who knows?" he asked, but clearly didn't care.

The throng of people formed a long line outside the ballroom. "I wonder why this line is moving so slowly," Coco said.

"Because one of the perks is the opportunity to meet the royal family just inside the door," Benjamin said in a dry tone.

"How do you know that?"

"One of the servers told me," he said.

Coco was tempted to bolt. She wasn't interested in having her bad curtsey viewed by so many people, and she could tell that Benjamin was bored out of his mind. "You're hating every minute of this, aren't you?"

"Well, it's not a ball game or a barbecue," Benjamin said. "I'm trying to look at it as a trip to the circus."

Coco laughed. "I like the idea of the circus."

"It's not just an idea," Benjamin said. "Look at how all these people are dressed. Feathers?"

"You could say the same about me," she said. "I. Sparkle. Kind of." She glanced down at the broach between her breasts.

He shook his head. "You look beautiful. No feathers. No way you look like a freak."

She smiled up at him. "Well, I guess that means I should thank you, though I'm not feeling overly flattered."

Benjamin leaned toward her. "You look damn good," he whispered in her ear.

"Thanks," she whispered. "You look pretty damn good yourself."

"It's the hat," he said.

"Yeah, and Emma would totally agree," Coco shot back.

He frowned at her.

"It's true," she said. "You and your Stetson. Scary."

"I'll make you change your mind," he said, ushering her closer to the doorway into the ballroom.

Finally, Coco was presented to Stefan and Eve. She curtsied. Again, awkwardly.

Stefan nodded and extended his hand. "I'm glad you could attend tonight. I hope you're enjoying yourself."

"Thank you for inviting me," Coco said.

"My pleasure. I'm grateful for your positive words to my wife," he said.

Coco nodded. "I wish you both the best," she said and was led to Eve.

"Good to see you," Eve said. "I love it that you curtsey the same way I did," she said with a chuckle.

"I suspect that's not a compliment on my form," Coco said.

Eve nodded. "But your advice to me was superior," she said.

"How are you feeling?" Coco asked.

"Good right now. I'm taking advantage of my good moments then resting during my other times. Thank you for coming tonight," Eve said and turned to Benjamin. "And you, too. You're a lucky man to have Coco."

Benjamin slid his hand around Coco's waist and nodded. "That, I am."

They were led away from Eve. Hating her instant emotional reaction to his touch, Coco moved away from him as soon as possible.

"You're going to need to pretend a little better," he said in a low voice next to her ear.

Again, his closeness made all her nerve endings jump. "I guess I'm not as good at pretending as I hoped I'd be."

"Looks like they have a good spread of food. Maybe that will make you feel better. I think there's even some chocolate. I'll get you a glass of champagne," he offered and walked toward a server.

Coco immediately felt a sliver of relief that he'd stepped away from her. She needed to get better control of her reactions to him. Coco didn't want to make a fool of herself over her boss. She tried to distract herself with the beautiful display of appetizers and desserts.

Benjamin returned with her champagne as she nibbled on a few bites of a crab cake. Seconds later, a band began to play. "Ladies and gentleman, I present Her Highness Bridget and her husband, Dr. Ryder McCall. Let the dancing commence."

Several couples immediately joined Princess Bridget and her husband on the dance floor. Coco watched, entranced by the scene. It was like something out of an enchanted story, more beautiful than any movie could capture. The women's dresses reflected the light from the chandeliers, and the men looked so handsome and sophisticated. Their reflections echoed off the mirrors on the walls of the ballroom.

"Wanna dance?" Benjamin asked.

Coco whipped her head around to look at him. "No," she immediately said.

"You look like you do," he said with a shrug.

"It's just so beautiful. All of it. The people, the women's dresses, the mirrors and the lights. Have you ever seen anything like it?"

He glanced at the dance floor. "It's a sight to see. I've been to a few charity events in Dallas where everyone was dressed in designer clothing and the rooms were decorated. Gotta say, though, I like the view from my backdoor on a spring morning better than this."

His comment took her by surprise, yet resonated inside her. For all the glamour and sophistication of her half siblings' lives, Coco felt so much more at ease back at the ranch. "You could be right," she said. "The flowers on the tables are beautiful, but nothing beats bluebells."

"Tough, but beautiful," Benjamin said. "Just like a Texan woman. C'mon and dance," he said, slipping his hand to her waist. "I'll never forgive myself if you didn't take your chance to dance at the palace."

She thought about refusing. Being close to Benjamin was hard on her. But how could she turn down the chance for this kind of memory? When would she ever get this opportunity again?

"Okay," she said and to her surprise, the band slid into a song just right for a Texas two-step. "A two-step," she said, stepping into Benjamin's arms and matching his rhythm. "How did that happen?"

"The international prompt," he said with a sly grin. "A tip to the right guy."

She couldn't help laughing at his confidence. Her heart shouldn't feel as if it was flying above her. She shouldn't feel as if she were ten feet off the ground. Shouldn't, shouldn't, shouldn't.

Just this once, Coco told her brain to stop and focused on the moment. Everyone and everything in the room was a blur to her except for Benjamin's deep gaze and his strong arms. She wondered if she would ever feel like this again.

After they danced, she indulged in a second glass of champagne. She allowed Benjamin to talk her into another head-spinning, heart-turning dance. Being held by him was addictive. She loved the scent of his soap and the sensation of his muscles beneath his jacket. His broad shoulders and slightly calloused hands provided a constant reminder that he was all male. And she was all female. His gaze was focused totally on her, and he drew her closer than was necessary.

Fighting giddiness, she excused herself to the powder room and washed her hands with cool water. She needed to dial down her reaction to him. He was just pretending, she reminded herself. Though true, the thought depressed her and she struggled with opposing feelings. Could he look at her that way, as if she were the most beautiful woman in the room, and truly feel nothing?

"Have you heard there's an illegitimate Devereaux here tonight?" one woman said to the other as they checked their makeup in the mirror.

Coco stopped cold and tried not to look in the women's direction.

"I'm surprised they're even recognizing her," the other woman said.

"She probably wants a handout. I heard it from a friend of Stefan's assistant that they're just being nice to her so she won't talk bad about them to the press. Any inheritance she receives will be a pittance."

"She's American, isn't she? I'll bet she'll try to get a reality show out of it. Low-class shows."

She looked in the mirror at herself and saw a woman with flushed cheeks and slightly tousled hair. A woman full of wishes and dreams she'd tried to deny. She'd been able to dismiss what was said by her distant cousin, Rodney. He'd seemed liked he delighted in scandalous news about the Devereaux. She supposed most people did, including the two women who'd just been talking about rumors. When more than one person was repeating the same rumor, though, maybe it wasn't a rumor. Maybe it was the truth. And maybe she was being a total fool to think that the Devereaux cared about her one little bit.

Suddenly, she couldn't bear to stay in the palace one more minute. It felt false and she felt silly. She had to get away. Leaving the powder room, she immediately caught sight of Benjamin and walked toward him.

"I'm ready to go, please," she said.

He studied her for a moment. "You're upset. What happened?"

"I just realized I don't belong here. The Devereaux aren't really my family, and they never will be."

"Are you sure?"

"Yes. Very sure," she said and pushed back the urge to cry. Her magical night at the palace was fake in every way. Since the Devereaux were all busy with guests, Coco thanked the official palace rep at the door. A car quickly arrived to take her and Benjamin back to the villa.

They arrived in no time and the nanny reported that Emma had easily fallen asleep. Coco felt like crap. All she wanted to do was ditch her dress and go to sleep. Maybe she could resell the dress on eBay. She felt weak and weepy and hated herself for it.

"I guess we should go to bed," she said and turned toward the hallway.

Benjamin caught her hand. "Come back."

"Not a good idea," she said in a voice that sounded husky to her own ears.

"You can trust me," he said and pulled her around to face him. "What's going on?"

She bit her lip, her stomach knotting. "It's all so fake. They don't want me here. You're not really my fiancé. It's too much."

He nodded and pulled her against him. "You've had a crazy time."

She buried her head in his chest and inhaled his wonderful scent that made her dizzy.

She forced herself to pull back. "I hate that it's all fake. The Devereaux want me to disappear. You don't really want me. I just want something real right now."

He paused a long moment, but kept her in his arms. "I want you," he confessed. "I just know I shouldn't."

"But you turn it off so easily," she said.

He lifted his forefinger to her lips. "Not really."

Her heart fluttered. "You could have fooled me."

His expression softened. "Sweetheart, you're easy to fool."

She took a deep breath. "Well, now, that really makes me feel better."

He lifted his hands to cradle her head. "Shut up," he whispered and lowered his head.

His lips landed on hers and she felt her consciousness begin to slide away. "I'm not sure," she said against his lips.

But he continued to kiss her, his tongue sliding past her lips. Tasting him, she had no inclination to pull away. Coco sank into him.

He slid his hand down her back to push her intimately against him.

"Oh, Benjamin, this is a bad—" She broke off when he rubbed against her. He was hard and wanting. Heat roared through her. Primitive need ricocheted through her bloodstream.

Coco craved more. She wanted all of him.

He squeezed her hips and groaned, undulating against her.

"Benjamin," she whispered. "Don't take me half-way this time."

He stopped and she could almost feel him debating. Seconds later, he gave her a French kiss that took her around the world and ground himself against her intimately. "I want you," he muttered.

A few breaths later, her dress was discarded on the floor, along with her underwear. She tugged at his bolo and shirt, then his black slacks. Benjamin shoved off his jacket. His skin was hot against hers. She craved his strength. His muscles flexed in an almost involuntary motion.

Coco couldn't get close enough. He continued to kiss her, pulling her down on the couch. She rubbed her breasts against his chest, drinking in his moan. "You're so sweet," he said. "I can't get enough."

He flipped her over on the couch and thrust inside her.

Coco gasped at the sensation.

"What?" he asked. "Don't tell me you're a virgin."

"No," she said. "It's just been a long time. And you're..."

"I'm what?" he prodded.

"Nothing," she managed. "Don't stop."

Benjamin couldn't seem to refuse the invitation. He began to pump and she echoed his movements. It was the most primitive, sensual experience she'd ever had. Coco just hoped it was more than physical for him, because it seemed to permeate her entire being. She was in deep trouble if this was just sex for him.

He thrust inside her and she could see his pleasure stamped on his face as he jerked and went over the top. It rocked her into another universe. She didn't climax, but something inside her would never be the same, and she curled around him and held him as tight as she could.

Chapter Ten

"You didn't come," he said, his eyes dark with sex and satisfaction.

"It's not important," she said because the experience had been so powerful for her. "Just being with you—"

Benjamin slid his hand between her legs and began to caress her.

"Oh," Coco said. "That feels—"

He found her sweet spot and she couldn't speak. It felt so good. She wriggled against his hand.

Moments later, he slid inside her again, hard and ready.

Coco stared at him in surprise. "What?"

"Yeah," he said and drove inside her.

Her breath caught and she left her inhibitions behind.

At this moment, Benjamin was everything. "Give yourself to me," he whispered. "All of you."

He continued to stroke her as he thrust inside her. Coco lost all concept of time. She gave herself totally to him.

She felt herself explode in a million sensations. Clinging to him, she pulled him into her.

She heard him swear six ways from Sunday. Finally, he slumped against her, still inside her.

"Lord help us," he said.

"Yeah," she whispered in response because she feared she would never get enough of him.

She felt Benjamin's release. A moment later, he began to stroke her in her most sensitive place. "Oh," she said. "I'm not sure—"

She broke off when she felt a twist of sensation.

"Give it to me," he said in a husky voice. "Give me all of you."

She couldn't refuse him. Between the way he touched her and the sound of his voice, she was all his. Coco gave herself to him and to the moment and went over the top.

Seconds, breaths later, she clung to him. "You're the most incredible woman in the world," he said, one hand cupping her jaw.

"Will you say that tomorrow?" she asked. "Or will you forget?"

His eyes blazed into hers. "I'll never forget."

* * *

Hours later, Emma cried out, waking both of them. Benjamin lifted his head. "I'll get her."

"No, I'll get her," Coco said, shaking her head and trying to clear her bleary vision.

"I can get her," he said and began to rise, naked from the bed.

"You might want to get a robe or something first," she managed.

He swore under his breath and groped around the room.

Coco found one of his shirts, and pulled it on. He was so much taller it almost reached to her knees. "Beat ya," she said and couldn't swallow a laugh.

She kissed him as Emma's cries grew louder. "Whatever you do, don't you dare tell me you regret this," she said, then rushed to Emma's room and grabbed a diaper and wipes. She found the baby howling and kicking.

"Well, good morning, sunshine," she said. "What's all this fussing for?" she asked as she changed Emma's diaper. Emma's cries faded as Coco chatted with her. Carrying the baby to the kitchen, she found Benjamin already warming a bottle. He'd pulled on a pair of jeans and a shirt he hadn't bothered to button. His hair was ruffled and when he looked at her, she wondered how a man holding a baby bottle could look so dangerously sexy.

"You get your shower. I'll take her," he said, extending his arms.

"Are you sure? She definitely woke up in a cranky-pants mood." She glanced at Emma who was studying Benjamin with a solemn gaze.

"She'll get over her reservations with me once I give her the bottle," he said in a dry tone. "Now go get your shower and get dressed, or I'll be tempted to take you back to bed."

Startled, she met his gaze and felt a rush of heat. "Is that a promise?"

He chuckled, taking the baby from her hands. "The first time I saw you, I thought you were the sweet, nurturing type. You looked so young I almost thought you were a teenager."

"But I'm not that young," she insisted.

"No. And you've got some fire underneath all that sweetness. I'll see you after you get dressed," he growled.

Delighted by the fact that he was finally seeing her as a woman, Coco hummed on her way to the shower. Benjamin couldn't deny that he had feelings for her now. He had shown her in a way no woman could mistake last night. They'd made no promises to each other, though. She needed to remember that. The thought almost made her stop humming, but Coco had never known a man like Benjamin and she suspected that she never would again. She just wouldn't count on anything between them lasting forever. That was okay, she told herself. No one in her life had been around forever.

Benjamin patted Emma's back after her feeding, and she let out a burp that would rival what he would expect from a truck driver. The fact that such a little being could let out such a loud sound never ceased to amaze him. "Bet you feel better, don't you?" he said, grinning at his daughter.

She giggled in return.

Her smile gave him a crazy little thrill. Thank goodness for Coco. He wondered if Emma would still be terrified of him if not for Coco. And now that he'd had Coco in his bed, things were definitely complicated. He couldn't deny a ferocious attraction for his daughter's nanny, but he also knew he wasn't in love. Even though Coco had insisted that he not voice his regrets, he knew he would have a hard time not thinking about her in a sexual way. And he feared that Coco, with her tender heart, might fall for him.

His phone rang, interrupting his worrisome thoughts. "Benjamin Garner," he said, propping Emma on his knee.

"This is Ray McAllister. Sorry to bother you, but I have some bad news. Foreman Hal broke his leg and had to have surgery. It will be a while before he'll be mobile again," he said. "Plus Jace quit yesterday."

Benjamin winced. "Damn. When it rains," he said and didn't need to finish the statement. "Is Hal okay?"

"More ticked off than anything else," he said.

"Okay. I'll make arrangements to get back to the ranch. Can you handle things until I get there?"

"Sure, boss."

"Okay, well, call if you have any problems. I'll be in touch," he said and turned off the phone.

Coco entered the room. "Problem?"

Benjamin nodded. "I have to get back to the ranch as soon as possible. My foreman broke his leg. You can stay here if you want."

She shook her head. "I think I've had enough of the Devereaux circus. I wouldn't have minded meeting my blood brother, but it looks like he doesn't care that much about meeting any of us. Maybe that's for the best. I'll pack."

Benjamin arranged for the flight and their palace rep took them to the airport. Coco had put together a carry-on bag to keep Emma fed, amused and happy, but he was hoping the baby would sleep.

He noticed that Coco stared out the window until the island of Chantaine disappeared from sight. "Are you sure you didn't want to stay?"

She shook her head. "No. My tie to the Devereaux is just an interesting story, and that's all."

"You keep saying that," Benjamin said. "I thought you and the princesses were starting to get along. They were nice to you, weren't they?"

"Yes, but I have reason to believe that the only reason they were nice is because they were afraid I would say bad things about them to the press."

"What makes you think that?"

"I overheard some ladies talking while I was in

the powder room," she said. "A man, he said he was a cousin. He pretty much said the same thing," she said.

"It doesn't matter why the Devereaux decided to be nice to you. It's important that they were. You wanted a chance to spend time with them and get to know them a little bit. So you got what you wanted," he said.

Coco frowned. "I would have preferred that they act more genuine to me."

"Not me. I wasn't going to let them be rude to you. You've gone through enough because of them. The least they could do is treat you with a little kindness."

Coco shook her head. "What do you mean *you* weren't going to let them be rude to me? You didn't have anything to do with how they acted toward me." Realization crossed her face. "Or did you?"

Benjamin shrugged. "It wasn't a big deal. I just had a little conversation with Stefan—"

Her eyes rounded. "Stefan," she echoed. "What kind of little conversation?"

"I just told him that you deserved better treatment than what you got at that tea party, and it could turn into a PR disaster if his family didn't act nicer," he said.

"So it's true?" she said. "The only reason they were friendly to me was because you threatened them."

"I didn't threaten," Benjamin said. "I just gave them facts. If they were snooty to you, and reporters asked about your time in Chantaine, you wouldn't have much good to say about the Devereaux."

"I can't believe you did that," she said in a harsh whisper.

"I can't believe you're getting all worked up over it," he said. "I was not going to allow them to make you feel like you're their daddy's dirt, because you're not. You're better than that."

Coco looked out the window. "I just wanted it to be as real as possible."

"Sweetheart, you're dealing with royals. They've spent most of their lives pretending."

"But I didn't want them to pretend with me."

Benjamin's gut twisted. Twice. She went silent and turned away from him.

Eleven long hours later, they arrived in Dallas, gritty-eyed and exhausted. One of his assistant foremen, Ray, greeted them after they picked up their luggage.

Benjamin sat in the front while Coco and Emma sat in the back of the SUV. Emma began to fuss and Coco gave her a bottle of diluted juice. Emma sucked it down in no time and gave one of her hearty burps. It must have been enough to tide her over, however, because she stopped whining.

"Fill me in," Benjamin said to his assistant foreman.

Ray did, and the news wasn't all that pretty. Benjamin had several full days of work ahead of him. Less than an hour later, they pulled into his ranch's driveway. Benjamin unfastened Emma's car seat and carried her inside.

"I'll take care of her," Coco said.

"The time change may have messed her up," he said.

"The time change will have us all messed up," she said with a tired smile.

"Yeah, I guess so," he said and lowered his head to kiss her. It wasn't a publicly necessary kiss. It was just something he was compelled to do. He felt her breathless surprise and took her mouth. It was an indulgence he allowed himself because he knew he would work nearly nonstop during the next few days.

He pulled back slightly. "Listen, about my talking to Stefan about you. No self-respecting fiancé would do less."

She studied his face. "I wouldn't know."

"Well, you do now," he said, and kissed her again.

It took over twenty-four hours for Coco and Emma to begin to recover from the time change. Half the time, when Emma was awake, Coco rested the baby on her chest. Two days later, she took Emma for a stroll around the house. Then another. And another.

At that point, it occurred to Coco that Emma needed exercise more than she did. She took the baby inside and set her down on a blanket for baby aerobics. Emma didn't enjoy the session. She cried until Coco rolled her onto her back and entertained her with toys. After several moments of more baby aerobics, Emma wailed for a few more moments.

Then Emma sank back against her baby pad and closed her gorgeous baby eyelids. "Well, that's my sign,"

Coco murmured and picked up the baby and carried her to her crib. Seconds later, Coco climbed into her own bed.

A few hours later, she awakened in the middle of the night. She rushed into the nursery to find Benjamin walking the floor with Emma.

Her heart leapt. “Sorry,” she said. “I can take over now.”

“I’m good,” he said. “How has she been since we got back?”

“I took her for a long walk, but she needed a workout,” she said.

He looked at her as he jiggled her while he walked. She rested her mouth on his shoulder. “She’s drooling. Is she teething?”

“Probably,” Coco said. “You’re good at that bobbing thing.”

He shot her a wry glance. “Think so?”

“Yeah. How was life on the ranch today?” she asked.

“Coulda been worse. There’s always catch-up when you go away. That’s probably why my father never took a vacation.”

“Do you regret the trip?” she asked.

“Not really,” he said. “I danced with the most beautiful woman in the world in Chantaine.”

She couldn’t help smiling all over. “That’s pretty darn nice.”

“Just telling the truth. Go back to bed.”

“I feel guilty,” she said.

"You won't in the morning when she wakes up screaming for a bottle."

Well, it had been a long several days, especially over the Atlantic. Which had been Benjamin's indulgence of her. "Sure?" she asked.

He nodded. "Go to bed."

She did as he suggested because she knew the next several days would be uncertain at best. When Coco awakened in the morning, she waited for the sound of Emma screaming, but there was only silence. Coco wasn't sure whether to relax or panic. She sat up in her bed and listened as she took a deep breath. Silence. No sound of Emma screaming or unhappy.

Rising from her bed, and still listening, she cracked open her bedroom door, but she still heard nothing. She feared not taking the opportunity to take a shower, but couldn't stop herself from listening for Emma. It was instinctive.

After several more moments of silence, Coco dove into the shower and washed herself from head to toe. She scrubbed herself dry, pulled on her clothes and went downstairs to find Emma in a high chair in the kitchen and Sarah spilling more Cheerios on her tray.

Emma picked up as many of the cereal bits as she could and stuffed them into her mouth.

"Take it easy," Sarah said. "You're not that hungry, sweetie. You put that fist in your mouth and you'll choke. Fact of life."

Coco winced and went toward the kitchen. Emma

began to choke. "Sarah," Coco said. Both of them tugged Emma's fist from her mouth.

"Emma, don't do that to yourself," Coco said.

"Learn this lesson young," Sarah said. "You can't eat more than you can fit in your mouth."

Coco decided an outing was in order. After breakfast, she plunked Emma into the stroller, then into the car seat and drove into town. She wheeled Emma through a discount store then went to the diner where her friend was serving several guests.

Coco asked to be led to a booth in the back and requested hot cocoa with marshmallows. A moment later Kim plopped down her hot chocolate along with applesauce and a spoon. "Back in a minute," Kim said.

"I'll be here." Coco sipped her hot chocolate and spoon-fed Emma.

The baby accepted the applesauce. "Good girl," she said as she stole a sip of hot chocolate.

Kim slid into the booth seat across from her. "Hello? So you're a princess? Why didn't you tell me?"

"Trust me. I'm no princess," Coco said and gave Emma another spoonful of food.

"But you went to Champagne," Kim said.

"Chantaine," Coco corrected. "I'd never heard of it, either."

"What were they like?" Kim asked.

Coco took a deep breath. She had to decide what she was going to say about the Devereaux. Now. She decided to go with the truth. "They were very kind to me," Coco said. "They work hard. They have children and husbands and they worry just like you and I do."

Kim frowned. "No dirt?"

Coco shook her head. "No dirt. They were nice."

"Well, that's boring," Kim said.

Coco laughed. "Sorry. You wanted me to have a miserable time?"

Kim rolled her eyes. "Of course not. I just thought it would be more exciting. Wasn't there anything exciting about the trip?"

"The island was beautiful. The beach was lovely. I got a great pair of shoes that I left in the villa where we stayed."

"Villa?" Kim echoed.

"House," Coco said. "We didn't stay at the palace. I went to tea and spilled mine on the tablecloth. Benjamin and I attended a gala at the palace."

"Oh, the gala must have been fabulous," she said with a dreamy look in her eyes. "Speaking of Benjamin, though, I understand you're engaged. Tell me more."

Coco gave a tentative nod. "It just happened. We're taking it slow," she said.

"Hmm," Kim said, lifting her eyebrow. "That sounds mysterious."

"It's not," Coco said. Emma let out a yell, bless her heart. "Oops, I think she wants more applesauce," she said and shoved another spoonful into the baby's open mouth.

"She is so cute," Kim said. "Do you want anything else for her?"

"I'm packing cereal, so I'm good," she said.

"You're so smart. You could be a mom," Kim said. "Gotta go."

Coco sighed as Kim walked away. For now, she had decided not to think about her connection to the Devereaux. Before, she couldn't help hoping for some great connection with the family who shared her father's genes and blood. The truth, however, was that they were all just people and, in her case, they had no bonds of history. She was truly alone in the world now, and she needed to make her peace with that.

Emma opened her mouth for more applesauce. Coco fed the baby several more spoonfuls. "Yummy, huh?" she asked and wiped off Emma's face.

Emma squawked, but permitted the cleanup. "Time to go," she said and lifted her from the high chair. She left extra money on the table for the bill and tip and headed out the door, waving at Kim as she left.

As she stepped outside the door, several people greeted her with microphones and cameras. "Miss Jordan, tell us about your experience in Chantaine. How did your sisters and brothers treat you? When will you be seeing them again?"

Emma curled against her in fear. "The Devereaux were very kind and welcoming to me. They could not have treated me better. The royal family works hard for the people of Chantaine, and they are just lovely." She paused a half beat as she heard the cameras flash. "That is all I have to say."

"But, Miss Jordan, what about your relationship with the Devereaux? What about—"

"That is all I have to say. I've responded to you. Now, you're frightening Emma. Please respect my privacy," she said, and walked to her car and put Emma into her safety seat. She got into the driver's seat and headed back to the ranch, jittery all the way.

When she pulled to the side of the house, Emma was fully asleep. Coco was relieved that the baby had not been traumatized by the experience, but it bothered her that the paparazzi had surprised her. She was still upset by it.

Coco took Emma inside, set her down in her crib for a nap and went to her own bed for a rest. For the first thirty minutes, her mind whirled. She remembered how Emma's body had tensed against hers in fear as the reporters surrounded them. The memory made her sick. More than anything, she wanted Emma to feel secure. She hated the idea that she was causing any kind of stress for the baby who had already lost her mother. Although she was exhausted, she tossed and turned, but finally fell asleep.

It must have been five minutes later that she heard Emma screaming at the top of her lungs. Coco nearly levitated from the bed. She glanced at the clock. It hadn't been five minutes. It had been *nearly an hour.* She collided with Benjamin as she raced into the nursery. "Sorry," she murmured. "I guess I was sleepier than I thought."

"Understandable," Benjamin said. "We're all still adjusting to the time change."

"I guess," Coco said and reached for Emma. "How are you, sweetie? Are you still frightened from this afternoon?"

"What happened this afternoon?" Benjamin asked as Coco changed Emma's diaper.

"I went to town, stopped at the diner, and a bunch of reporters and photographers were waiting outside. I think they scared Emma because she was wrapping herself around me like a rubber band."

Benjamin frowned. "I would have thought the fuss would have died down by now."

"You and me both," Coco said and held Emma against her. "I decided to give a positive statement about the Devereaux. Nothing more, but of course, they wanted more."

Benjamin sighed. "I guess I'll just have to keep one of my men available for you."

Coco felt guilty. She knew that Benjamin had lost two of his top employees. "That doesn't seem fair," she said. "I don't think it's right that you should have to give up one of your employees because of me."

Benjamin shrugged. "You gotta do what you gotta do. Other than the scare today, how's she's doing?"

"She's getting more interested in sounds. I think she may try to communicate even more soon."

"Seems to me she communicates pretty strongly when she screams," Benjamin said in a wry voice. At the same time, he lifted his hand to the baby's hand. Emma curled her fist around his finger. "So tiny. So vulnerable. Keeping her safe scares the hell out of me sometimes."

"You're doing a pretty good job," Coco said as she slid her hand over his.

He met her gaze for a long moment. "So are you. I've missed you."

Her heart skipped over itself. "I've missed you, too," she whispered.

"Ranch demands have been crazy since I got back," he said.

"I know," she said. "It was a luxury for you to go to Chantaine with me. I still appreciate it."

"Even though you didn't want me talking to Stefan on your behalf," he said.

"Well," she said and took a deep breath, "I think you were operating in my best interests."

"I didn't want to have to beat him up for him to see the truth," he said, sliding his hand over her hair.

"You would have been arrested for that," she said.

Benjamin shrugged. "Sometimes you gotta do what you gotta do. Listen," he said. "Ask Sarah for help. She's okay with it, and Emma doesn't mind her."

Coco nodded. "I'll work on it. I just don't want to overwork Sarah. She has a lot to do, preparing meals for your staff."

"Yeah, but she took advantage of the time we were away. With a baby in the house, we all have to make adjustments and Sarah knows that, too."

"Okay," she said.

"And I'll assign one of my men to you," he said.

"That shouldn't be necessary," she said. "I don't go out that often and I don't like the idea of pulling someone away from their assignments just because I want to go into town."

"I'll give you a cell number. Let him know when you want to go out and he'll escort you. It won't be a big deal," Benjamin said.

"Are you sure?" she asked, skeptical.

"Yeah. Now don't argue with me. There are times when my guys are sitting around doing nothing. You're just making one of them earn his pay every now and then."

"If you say so," she said.

"I am," he said and lowered his mouth to hers, taking her in a long kiss that reminded her of the night they'd shared at the villa in Chantaine.

Chapter Eleven

Although it was a bit chilly outside, Coco bundled up the baby and took her for a stroll. Emma really seemed to enjoy the outdoors. After she returned it was dinnertime, and she fed the baby then bathed her and put her to bed after one more bottle. As much as Coco had needed that little nap she took earlier, she knew it would be a while before she would be tired enough to sleep tonight, so she put on a jacket and went for another walk around the house.

After she'd made two and a half circles, Benjamin appeared at her side. "So, what's bothering you now?"

"Nothing," she said, thinking she was most bothered by the warm pleasure she felt just having him by her side. "I guess I was caught off guard at the diner today, but I'm hoping the interest will die down now."

"It will," he said. "What else?"

"Nothing. I'm just trying to burn off some extra energy, so I'll be able to sleep tonight."

"I would have thought Emma would take care of burning off any extra energy," he said.

She chuckled. "She usually does, but since I took that late nap…"

He stepped in front of her and pulled her against him, and looked down at her from beneath his hat. He pushed a strand of hair from her face. "I can help you burn off your extra energy," he offered in a low voice that made her heart stutter.

His suggestion was unmistakably sexual. Her nerve endings hummed. "What about Sarah?" she asked because the housekeeper lived in a small suite downstairs.

"Sarah will be too busy watching her reality television to notice," he said. "I haven't stopped thinking about being with you."

Coco hadn't stopped thinking about him, either. "Okay," she whispered because her throat was tight with anticipation. "How— Where—" She shrugged.

"Your room," he said. "You go upstairs first. I'll be up in five minutes or less," he promised then lowered his head to kiss away any reservations.

Her heart hammering, she strode quickly to the house, then upstairs to her bedroom. Pulling off her jacket, she wondered if she should change clothes. She didn't have any sexy lingerie. She started to panic, but then he opened the door and closed it behind him.

"Nervous?" he asked as he walked toward her.

"A little," she admitted.

"Or excited," he said with a sexy grin.

"Maybe," she said, wishing she had half his confidence. "What about you?"

He gently pushed her down on the bed with his arm beneath her to cushion her fall. He followed her down. "I'm not at all nervous," he said and when she felt his hard lower body against hers, his arousal was unmistakable.

Then he kissed her and everything blurred deliciously together. He helped her remove her clothes. She awkwardly helped with his. His hands heated her skin everywhere he touched her. She relished the sensation of his muscular body entwined with hers. He touched and teased her and she did the same to him until they couldn't stand the anticipation one second longer. He drove her over the edge and he followed.

Benjamin rolled to his side, panting after his release. Pulling her against him, he nuzzled her head with his chin. "I can't get enough of you. How'd you do that?" he asked.

She smiled into his throat. "Same, same," she said. "I lo—" He stiffened and she broke off in horror because she'd almost said she *loved* him. "I—" She cleared her throat. "I really like being with you," she said. "In every way."

She felt his body relax against hers. "I feel the same way," he said and rubbed his mouth down her cheek to her lips.

The next morning, she awakened to the sound of Emma chatting through the baby monitor. And no Benjamin beside her. She felt an odd sense of loss and confusion but pushed it aside as she pulled on a long-sleeved T-shirt, underwear and a pair of jeans. Walking into the nursery, Coco found Emma batting at a stuffed bunny and chatting with it.

Coco's heart twisted in love. Emma had grown so much since the first day she'd taken over as nanny. "Hello, Miss Chatterbox. How are you this morning?"

Emma immediately turned her head to look at Coco and gave her a toothless smile.

"Aren't you the gorgeous one?" she said and changed the baby's diaper. She lifted her up from her crib and pointed to Benjamin's photograph on the chest of drawers. "That's your daddy. Can you say daddy?"

Emma made several unintelligible sounds.

"Da-da," Coco said. "Da-da, Da-da, Da-da." She'd coached the baby too many times to count.

Emma continued to make her sounds. Just as Coco began to turn away, the baby said, "Da-da."

Coco blinked. "Did you say Da-da?"

"Da-da-da-da," she repeated.

"You're saying Da-da," Coco said, so excited she couldn't stand it. "Da-da."

"Da-da-da-da," Emma said.

"Gotta find your daddy," Coco said and bolted for the stairs. She hoped Benjamin was in the office. Darting to the office door, she threw open the door, but he wasn't there. Her heart sank. "Dang." Searching her mind for a way to record the moment, she pulled her cell phone from her pocket and pushed record. "Say Da-da," she said holding the phone toward Emma's mouth.

Distracted by the phone, Emma leaned toward it and tried to lick it.

"No," Coco said and pulled the phone slightly away. "Da-da," she coached. "Da-da."

"Da-da," Emma whispered.

"Good girl," Coco said. "Again. Da-da."

"Da-da-da-da-da-da."

Coco saved the recording and kissed Emma on her cheek. "Yay."

After she gave Emma her bottle, Coco sent the voice recording to Benjamin's phone.

Moments later, he called her back. "Did I hear what I think I heard?"

"You did. Your daughter said Da-da. How does it feel?"

"Pretty damn good," he said. "Do you think she knows what she's saying?"

"Mostly," she said. "I point to your photo and say *Daddy*. She said it for the first time this morning. I'm excited."

Benjamin chuckled. "I can tell you are. Thanks for

the recording," he said. "And thanks for last night," he added.

"Sure," she said, her stomach taking a dip. "Sure. I'll talk to you later." She hung up the phone full of mixed feelings. Just hours ago, she and Benjamin had made love, but she could tell that he didn't want to hear her tell him she loved him. And just now, she was turning cartwheels because his daughter had uttered two identical syllables that may or may not identify him.

Her chest tightened with the realization that she was feeling too much for Benjamin. He might regard her as a fun lover, but he didn't truly want her as a fiancée, let alone as a wife.

She was his *employee.*

That knowledge stirred her uncertainties. How was she supposed to manage her growing feelings for Benjamin when they were living in the same house and he seemed more than happy to share her bed? On occasion, anyway. And what would happen to her when his desire for her waned?

Coco wasn't sure how to keep her heart safe. She was all alone in the world, and even though Benjamin had stepped up to help her, she shouldn't count on him. She shouldn't mistake his kindness and sexual interest for anything more.

The house phone began to ring again, calls for Coco, wanting her to make an appearance or give an interview. Coco could tell that Sarah was growing impatient with the interruptions.

After Emma's morning nap and lunch, Coco decided they could both use an outing. She knew of a park in town and although it was a little chilly, she thought she could bundle Emma well. And, heaven knew, she needed to get out. Her thoughts and feelings were ricocheting throughout her body and mind. She gave a call to the ranch hand Benjamin had assigned to her and left a message when he didn't answer.

She drove to the park, hauled out the stroller and plopped Emma into it. "Ready to go?" she said.

Emma, wrapped up with a hooded coat, looked around. Coco rose and found a group of photographers coming toward her. She held up her hand. "Whoa. Leave us alone."

"We just want to ask you more about your visit to Chantaine," a man said.

"I've already said all I'm going to say. The Devereaux were very kind to me and Chantaine is a beautiful island. I wish all of you would have the opportunity to visit. There's nothing else to say."

"There has to be more," a woman said, lifting a microphone in her direction.

"No, there's really nothing more to say," Coco said. "Now, please leave us alone."

"But—"

"But nothing," Coco said and shoved the stroller away from the paparazzi vultures. She practically ran and it wasn't a running stroller.

Emma giggled, and Coco wished she could laugh,

too, but she was so furious with the intrusion in her life. In Emma's life. In Benjamin's life. She would have thought all the craziness would have died down. But no. She wondered how long it would take. She wondered *what* it would take to make them stop.

Rounding a curve, a man leapt out in front of her. Coco screamed, and Emma began to cry.

"I just want an interview," the man said.

"Leave me and my—" She searched for the word, because they weren't her family. Brutal truth. Emma wasn't her baby. Benjamin and Sarah weren't her family, as much as she might want them to be. And Boomer wasn't her dog. "Leave my friends alone."

She ran away and prayed she wouldn't encounter anyone else.

Upset by the paparazzi, Coco struggled to figure out what she should do. It would be so much easier to just continue on her current path. Benjamin was more than happy with how she'd taken care of Emma. He was also happy to have her in his bed as long as deep emotions and true commitment weren't involved. That reality ripped at her.

So how did she take care of Benjamin and Emma and herself at the same time? Coco brooded over that question. What was best for Emma? What was best for Benjamin? What was best for Coco? The same answer kept coming back to her again and again, and Coco knew it would only cause her more pain. But it was all too necessary.

The next day, she advertised for a nanny.

Over the following week, she avoided Benjamin and interviewed her possible replacement. It sounded drastic, but Coco couldn't handle her feelings for Benjamin and she wanted the best for both Emma and her father. That meant she needed to leave. She would adjust to the change. She had to. She knew what it was to lose people she loved. Sometimes she wondered if that was her destiny.

Coco interviewed five women for her position. One was perfect. Coco insisted on two background checks that came back cleaner than a whistle. Susan Littleton was perfect. More perfect than Coco was, which made her feel oddly envious.

Despite her yuck feelings, she forged on and confronted Benjamin before he left one morning. "What's up?" he asked as she met him in the front room.

"I need to talk to you," she said.

"That's new," he said with a grumpy expression on his face. "You've been avoiding me."

"Yes. I'm sorry. I wanted to be with you, but—"

"Yeah, yeah," Benjamin said, clearly not believing her.

Coco took a deep breath. "I think it might be best if I leave."

Benjamin's eyes widened in alarm. "Why?"

"I can't stand the way the paparazzi are haunting

me, Emma, you," she said. "It's wrong. And I think the only way to make them go away is for me to go away."

"What?" he asked.

She bit her lip. "Yes, and then there's our so-called engagement," she said. "And the sex. I don't think I can handle sex and a nonengagement with you."

"Then we can stop," he said.

"Easy for you to turn off your emotions. Not for me," she said. "I really want to stay, but I want what's best for Emma. And you."

Benjamin's expression turned grim. "So what the hell do you think is *best* for Emma and me?"

Her stomach clenched at the hostility in his voice. She handed him the folder she'd held by her side. "I have found a wonderful replacement. She's probably even better than I am," she admitted reluctantly. "Her name is Susan Littleton and I've put her through numerous interviews and background checks."

"I don't have time for this," he said.

"She's already met Emma, and Emma loves her," Coco said.

"You're determined to do this," he said.

"I think it's best," she said, her heart breaking.

"I didn't think you would quit on us," he said and put his hat on his head. "I'll meet with her tomorrow," he said and walked out the front door.

The next day, the shoes Coco had left in Chantaine arrived with a note from Bridget. *I can't believe you left without saying goodbye. I can't believe you left without your Cinderella shoes. Yours truly, Bridget.*

Coco could almost believe Bridget was sincere. She could almost believe Bridget cared about her.

That would be a mistake, wouldn't it? She looked at the shoes and remembered dancing with Benjamin at the palace. Her heart twisted at the memory. She took the shoes to Emma's room and put them in the baby's closet. Maybe when she was older, she could use them when she played dress-up. It tore at her to know she would miss the precious milestones of Emma's growth.

After his own background investigation and interview, Benjamin reluctantly approved Susan Littleton. He was angry and upset that Coco was abandoning him. He'd grown to care for her, and God knew Emma adored her. He would have been far more terrified about Coco leaving if he hadn't observed Susan and Emma. He also knew, however, that Coco had been responsible for bringing Emma to the place that she could accept another caregiver.

His life was simple and the ranch could be boring for a woman. He couldn't help wondering if Coco shared some of his mother's qualities. Maybe she had a little wanderlust. That would explain her determination to leave.

Benjamin surrounded his heart and emotions with barbed wire. That way, no one could wound him. He helped Coco pack her small car. Reluctantly.

She placed one last box on her passenger seat and turned to face him.

"You're sure you want to do this?" he asked, shoving his hands into his pockets.

She took a deep breath and bit her lip. "I'm sure it's right for you and Emma."

He narrowed his eyes. "Is it that easy for you to leave?"

Her eyes turned dark with emotion. "Not at all. Just the right thing," she said. "Thank you for everything."

She hugged him and he couldn't quite resist embracing her in return. "Yeah," he said. "Don't be a stranger, princess."

She laughed. "That's such a joke," she said and pulled back. "Thank you again, for everything."

Coco got into her car and drove out of his life.

Coco didn't know where she was going. She just wanted to remove all the attention directed at her away from Benjamin and Coco. That was her goal. She should feel a great deal of satisfaction. And she did, she told herself. She really did.

So why did she also feel miserable?

Coco drove to Fort Worth and got a cheap hotel for the night. Although she'd carefully planned her exit, she hadn't planned what she would do next. Coco was at a loss. She considered making a trip to the Gulf Coast. With her car loaded with all her belongings, she wasn't sure that was practical.

When she awakened the next morning to silence and no baby sounds, sadness overwhelmed her. She missed Emma. She missed Benjamin. She glanced out the window at the gray day and fought tears. Trying to pull herself out of her misery, she took a shower then checked her phone. She'd received a voice message from a Valentina Devereaux Logan, telling her to call her back. To say the least, Coco was surprised by the message. During her continental breakfast provided by the hotel, she debated whether she should return the call.

Tossing a coin, she made the decision when tails won the call.

Coco dialed the number, braced for anything.

"Hello, Tina speaking," a woman said, as a child screamed in the background.

The sound of the screaming child somehow immediately put Coco at ease. After caring for Emma, it was such a familiar sound. "This is Coco Jordan."

"Oh, lovely," Tina said. "Pardon me for a moment. My daughter is being a tyrant. Katiana, you may not have cupcakes for breakfast, and if you continue to scream, you'll be sitting in the naughty chair."

Coco couldn't help smiling at Tina's words to her daughter.

"There now, again pardon me," Tina said. "I hear you're leaving your current position due to the paparazzi. You must come and stay with me."

Coco blinked. "Excuse me?"

"Yes, you must come here. After all, everyone, except one of my brothers and I, has met you. That's not at all fair, is it?"

"I wouldn't know," Coco said. "How did you know I'd left my job?"

"Bridget called and talked to the housekeeper. I would have called before, but Stefan was such a bear. Of course, now he thinks you walk on water since you got Eve to slow down a bit."

Coco took a deep breath, trying to stay on track with the conversation. "I really don't need your pity."

"Well, you've got it because I've suffered the paparazzi. But the real reason I want you to come is because I want to meet you. And I want to see your eyes. Bridget tells me you have the Devereaux eyes. But kinder."

"I don't know what to say," Coco said. She hadn't expected this at all.

"You should say, 'Yes, thank you very much. I'll accept your invitation,'" Tina said.

It wasn't as if she had anywhere else to go, Coco thought. "Maybe I could just visit for the day," she said, thinking out loud.

"Or longer," Tina said. "I'll give you the address so you can put it in your GPS, although you may have to call again once you get closer." Tina recited the address.

"If you're sure," Coco said.

"I'm quite sure and I look forward to meeting you," she said.

Coco followed the instructions to the ranch where

Valentina and her family lived. The main house was beautiful and there was a turkey wreath on the front door to add a homey touch. Standing on the front porch as she knocked on the door made her homesick for Benjamin's ranch.

She heard a rush of footsteps. "Katiana, heavens child," a woman said and opened the door. A middle-aged woman with iron-gray hair and a little girl with brown curly hair pulled into pigtails stood in front of Coco.

"You must be Coco Jordan. I'm Hildie and this is Katiana. Come on in. Her Highlyness is on the phone about another one of her charity projects. She's determined to save the world," the woman said as she led Coco inside the house to a den furnished with comfortable-looking furniture and toys on the floor. "She'll be right with you. In the meantime, Katiana, you can pick up your toys and get ready for lunch."

"But I'm still playin'," the little girl said.

"I'll help," Coco offered.

Hildie glanced at her. "Hmm. That's nice of you," she said and left the room.

"What do we have here?" Coco asked Katiana.

The child picked up one of the figurines on the floor. "This is Rose the Fairy Queen. She's the boss of the other fairies."

"I'll bet she's very smart," Coco said. "Where does she take her nap?"

"In the box," Katiana said and stroked the fairy figurine. "But I like to take them with me when I nap sometimes."

"It's probably easier for everyone to get their sleep if they go in the box. Is this a pony fairy?" she asked, picking up a horse figurine.

Katiana nodded and began to tell a story about how the pony likes to take everyone for a ride. Coco couldn't help wondering if Emma would play with fairy dolls and make up stories about them. Within a few moments, and a few extra stories, the two of them got all the toys put away in the box.

A young woman with wavy brown hair and dressed in casual clothes entered the room. "Oh, no. Have we already put you to work?" she asked. "I'm Tina."

Coco stood, wondering for a moment if she should curtsey.

"Don't you dare curtsey," Tina said as if she'd read her mind and moved toward her, extending both her hands. "It was so lovely of you to come, Coco. And Bridget and Phillipa were right. Devereaux eyes, but so kind. You've met my daughter, Katiana," Tina said.

"Yes, she told me all about her flower fairies," Coco said. "She's so verbal."

Tina ruffled her daughter's hair. "Yes, a blessing or a curse depending on the moment. Miss Hildie is going to give you lunch while Coco and I have a chat."

"I want to chat, too," Katiana said.

"Later, if you take a good nap. Run along," she said and dropped a kiss on her daughter's cheek. "Please have a seat. Would you like something to drink? Tea, coffee, apple cider?"

"Apple cider would be great," she said and Hildie delivered mugs to each of them within moments.

"Now, I've heard a bit about you. You lost both parents and your mother was ill for some time. Please accept my condolences," Tina said, covering Coco's hand with her own. "I'm also terribly sorry you felt you needed to quit your job. And weren't you engaged to the ranch owner?"

Coco felt her cheeks heat. "It was more of an arrangement than a real engagement. He just offered to pretend in order to protect me from the crazy offers I was receiving. I thought it would all die down, but I couldn't take Emma for a stroll in the park without being hounded by the paparazzi. Emma had been through so much with losing her mother and coming to live with her father, and they didn't get along very well in the beginning at all."

"He didn't like the baby?" Tina asked, clearly appalled.

"Oh, no, he loved her. She was terrified of him, screamed every time he came around. But that's all better now. She even said *Da-da* the other day," Coco said. Then she took a breath. "But the paparazzi were causing too much of a burden on the whole household. It just didn't seem right to me that Benjamin would assign one of his men as a guard."

"So you quit because of the press?" Tina asked.

"Mostly. There was also some confusion over pretending to be engaged, and I didn't want to get into that kind of situation with my employer. Especially since I lived in his house, and—" She broke off. "I'm sorry. I'm rambling."

"Not at all," Tina said. "It must have been hard to leave the baby."

Coco felt tears sting her eyes and her heart swell with a knot of emotion. Tina was so kind and seemed so genuine that Coco felt as if she could be herself with the woman. "Terribly. The only consolation I have is that I found a wonderful nanny. She'll probably be better than I was," she said.

"Oh, I doubt that. So what are your plans?"

"I don't know. Get a job. I've thought about finishing my education. I only had a year and a half left when my mother got so ill," she said. "I couldn't imagine going back right away. There was so much that had to be done afterward."

"Of course you couldn't. But maybe you're a bit more ready. Hildie's very big on education. She always says that once you have your degree, no one can take it away from you," Tina said.

"Hildie sounds like a smart woman," Coco said.

"She's a treasure. I can't imagine our lives without her. As soon as I put down Katiana, you and I can have lunch. Chicken noodle soup. Would you like to freshen up? I can ask one of the ranch hands to bring in your luggage."

"Oh, no, that won't be necessary," Coco said, although the thought was tempting. Tina seemed to infuse the house with warmth and comfort.

"Well, you must stay at least one night because I've already promised Katiana you'll be around this afternoon. We can't have you driving around these country roads in the dark."

Coco stayed for lunch and dinner and met Zachary Logan, Tina's husband, who looked at his wife and daughter with such adoring eyes that it made Coco's heart hurt. She wondered if a man would ever look at her the same way. Coco knew she should have left when she did, because she had begun to wish that Benjamin would make their engagement real, and that had been a very dangerous wish. Being at the Logan ranch soothed her at the same time it reminded her of what she'd left behind.

Two days later, Coco felt she had accepted as much of Tina's hospitality as she should. She headed toward Fort Worth to apply for jobs and, if she was lucky, entrance into a university to complete her degree.

Chapter Twelve

Two and a half weeks later, Benjamin sat in his office and stared into a glass of whiskey. A knock sounded at the door. It was nearly 8:00 p.m. He knew it was Sarah. He opened the door and there she stood with a tray in her hands bearing a sandwich and soup. "Hi, Sarah. Thanks."

"You haven't been eating well," she said with a disapproving glance. "And you're drinking too much, too."

"Sarah," he said in a warning voice as he returned to his chair.

"Well, you are. It's not healthy. You're upset. It's not good for the baby," she said.

"What do you mean it's not good for Emma? She's fine. Susan is doing a great job."

"How much time have you been spending with your daughter?" Sarah demanded.

Benjamin hung his head. He'd buried himself in his work ever since Coco had left.

"You should go after that woman and make her come back," Sarah said. "Coco was the best thing that's happened to this house in a long time."

"You didn't feel that way when the phone was ringing off the hook with calls for her," he said, looking up at her.

Sarah waved her hand. "A minor annoyance."

"She's the one who left. She was determined to go," he said, plunging his spoon into his soup. He lifted it to his mouth and scalded his tongue. "Damn."

"That's what you get for not doing the right thing. If you hadn't let her get away, you wouldn't be in this situation," Sarah said, crossing her arms over her chest.

"How was I supposed to keep her when she wanted to leave?" he asked.

"Maybe you could have told her you had feelings for her," Sarah said.

"I never said that," he said, stirring his soup.

"Well, maybe you should have," she retorted. "You were engaged to her. Or at least you said you were."

Benjamin frowned at his housekeeper's razor-sharp instincts. She clearly thought there'd been something fishy about the engagement. "How do you know she wasn't getting bored? Maybe she has signed up for one of those reality TV shows or is taking all those interviews that she was offered," he said.

"She's in Fort Worth working as a waitress trying to go back to school in January," Sarah scoffed.

He stared at her. "How do you know that?"

"I have my ways," she said. "You messed up," she said, wagging her finger at him. "It's up to you to fix it."

He gave her his best scowl, but she was unmoved. "I have work to do," he said and looked at his laptop.

"Yes, you do. In more ways than one," she said and left the room.

Benjamin stared after her, then rose to close the door. There were definite downsides to having long-time employees. A. They thought they knew you better than they should know you. B. They thought they had the right to speak their mind.

Benjamin snarled and returned to his desk. He took bites of his sandwich and spoonfuls of soup. Thank goodness, the soup had cooled. Excel files faded before his eyes. Images of Coco stood front and center. He saw her smiling and laughing, kissing him. He saw her kissing Emma's head as she rocked her to sleep. He saw her falling for him.

Benjamin plunged his head into his hands. What could he do? What *should* he do?

Two days before Thanksgiving, Coco hustled to deliver blueberry pancakes at a Fort Worth café. After an afternoon break, she would serve T-bones at a popular steakhouse. If she was lucky, she would be able to get a loan for her first semester at a state-supported school within a couple weeks.

She automatically delivered water and coffee to two tables, took orders and placed them. After delivering orders to another table and picking up ketchup, hot sauce and extra butter, she grabbed a cup of water for the table in the back. "Would you like coffee?" she asked, her pitcher poised above the customer's cup.

"Always," he said. His voice was too familiar. She'd heard it in her dreams. She glanced up and stared into the dark-eyed gaze of Benjamin Garner.

"Hi," she managed, her heart racing in an irregular beat. "What are you doing here?"

"Needed some breakfast," he said and glanced at the menu.

"Oh," she said and pulled out her pad. "What would you like?"

"What's good?"

"Most everything," she said. "Blueberry and pecan pancakes are popular, along with the meat-eaters omelet."

He nodded. "You like this job better than taking care of Emma?" he asked.

Her heart fell and so did her cheery facade, but she quickly pulled it back in place. "Not really, but I needed to go." She took a deep breath to calm herself and lifted her pencil to her pad. "What do you want?"

"Eggs, bacon and pecan pancakes," he said.

"Can do," she said and turned away. Her heart was tripping over itself. She just prayed she wouldn't trip over her own feet. She'd never expected Benjamin to show up here, but then, she'd never expected to see him again in her life. Coco resisted the urge to rush to the bathroom and fix her hair or put on some lipstick. She knew what she looked like, and it wasn't at all glamorous.

Forcing herself to focus, she delivered orders to other tables and when Benjamin's order was ready, she placed it on his table, along with extra butter, syrup and orange juice.

"I didn't order orange juice," he said.

"It comes with the pancakes. Can I get you anything else?" she asked.

"Yes, you can," he said, locking his gaze with hers. "You can come back to the ranch with me."

She almost dropped her carafe of coffee, but clenched her fist. "I—um—I can't do that."

He rose to his feet. "Why not?"

She sucked in a deep breath. "It just wouldn't work. I started to feel too much—" She broke off. "Want too—" She shook her head, not wanting to reveal how deep her feelings for him were.

"You started to want me. You started to love me," Benjamin said.

She closed her eyes, trying to keep herself under control. "Don't be cruel," she whispered.

"I'm not being cruel," he said. "I started loving you, too."

Coco opened her eyes and gaped at Benjamin. The carafe dropped from her hand. She stared at the coffee spilling on the floor. "Darn."

"It's just coffee," Benjamin said and pulled her into his arms. "I love you. I want you in my life forever. I want you to marry me."

Coco met his gaze and felt her knees weaken. "Marry you?"

"Yeah," he said. "I know I can be a pain in the butt, but being with you makes me happier than I ever thought I could be. I've been a miserable fool since you left."

Coco bit her lip, feeling overwhelmed with emotion. "But I thought you weren't ready. I thought you didn't want to make a commitment," she said and he covered her lips with his fingers.

"I was wrong," he said. "Don't expect me to say that a lot," he told her. "But you took me by surprise. I didn't expect you to get under my skin, but I'm glad you did. I want you under my skin and in my life forever. Starting now. Marry me," he said and pulled a box from his pocket. "This time, for real," he said, and flipped open the box to reveal a diamond ring.

Gasping, Coco couldn't fight the tears burning her eyes. She looked into the gaze of the man who was everything she'd ever hoped for. "Yes," she said. "I love you."

"And I love you," he said.

* * *

A month later, just before Christmas, she and Benjamin, along with the new nanny, and Sarah, traveled to Chantaine. Bridget had insisted that Coco and Benjamin get married in Chantaine. At first, they had protested, but then they had both seen the wisdom of combining their wedding with a honeymoon. Coco had also realized that the Devereaux were far more welcoming to her than she had previously thought.

Eve, in full bloom of pregnancy, and Pippa, with her baby bump, fussed at her dress.

"It's beautiful," Eve said of Coco's shoulder-grazing lace dress. "And I'm not the prissy type."

"Neither am I," Pippa said. "And I love it, too. Benjamin's a lucky guy."

"Damn lucky," Bridget said, entering the room in five-inch heels. "The nannies are taking care of our lovely demons, so we should get this show on the road, as you Americans say."

Soon after, Valentina and Katiana entered the room above the chapel where Coco and Benjamin would soon be married. Tina moved toward Coco and embraced her. "You look gorgeous."

"Like a princess flower fairy," Katiana said.

Coco bent down to kiss Tina's daughter. "You are so sweet."

"Time to move out, everyone," Bridget said, clapping her hands as she toddled in her Christian Louboutin heels. "Can't keep the groom waiting forever."

Each of the Devereaux women kissed her on the cheek before they left. Bridget lingered behind. "You're a wonderful addition to our family," she said. "We're so lucky to have you."

Tears wells in Coco's eyes. "I'm the lucky one."

"We would all argue that, but not now," Bridget said and gently pressed a handkerchief underneath Coco's eyes. "Are you okay?"

"Yes, it's just been a journey. Less than a year ago, my mother died of cancer, penniless, then I became a nanny. After that, I went back to waitressing. Now I'm getting married to a man I was afraid to dream of. It's been a crazy year."

"And it's only going to get better," Bridget said with a mysterious glint in her eyes.

Coco wrinkled her brow. "What do you mean?"

"You'll see soon enough," she said. "Do you need anything else?"

"Just a little help getting down the stairs," Coco said.

Bridget opened the door and the wedding assistant appeared. "I am at your service, miss."

The assistant guided her down the stairs and Coco waited in the foyer for her cue to enter the chapel. Her stomach danced with nerves as the doors were thrown open and she walked, by herself, down the aisle.

Benjamin stood, in his Western tux, waiting for her at the front of the church. The other guests disappeared before her eyes. At this moment, Benjamin was her everything, and he held her gaze every step of the way down the aisle.

Coco finally arrived by his side and he took her hands and kissed her. "You're safe with me," he whispered. "You'll always be safe with me."

He couldn't have said anything that moved her more. He couldn't have said anything that made her feel she'd finally found home. With him.

The minister called the service to order.

Benjamin recited his vows. Coco made hers, and they were pronounced man and wife. The small group in the chapel applauded in approval, and Benjamin took her mouth in a kiss that sealed their promises for a lifetime. Coco swooned. Oh, how could that happen to a modern-day nonprincess?

After the ceremony, there was a private reception in a palace ballroom. Stefan took the stage. "We have the unusual joy of sharing the marriage of our father's daughter, Coco Jordan, to Benjamin Garner. In this unusual and blessed situation, the Devereaux family wishes to convey a special, honorary title to Coco. She has already contributed in a unique way to our family. That said, Coco Jordan is now Honorary Princess of Chantaine," he said and dipped his head. "Bless you and yours and forever."

Coco looked at Benjamin. "Did he just say what I thought he said?" she asked.

He chuckled and nodded. "He did."

"So I'm a princess?"

"You always were royalty in my eyes," he joked, his gaze holding hers.

She laughed and shook her head. "I didn't need to be a princess. I just needed to belong to you."

He took her mouth in a kiss. "Looks like I'll have to hire an extra guy to protect my princess. No worries, darlin'. You're worth every penny."

Coco sank into him. "I'm the luckiest girl in the universe."

"Just one more thing," Bridget said, interrupting their kiss as she led a tall man toward her. "Eve helped. We did something similar for her."

Coco pulled back, studying Bridget and the tall man. Something about him seemed familiar. She stared at him and noticed that his eyes mirrored hers in color. Her heart reverberated in recognition.

"You're my brother, aren't you?" she asked.

"Yes. And you're my sister," he replied. "Maxwell Carter at your service, Your Highness," he said with a wry grin.

She laughed out loud. "Yes, just as you are a prince. Your Highness."

"Not me," he said with a shake of his head. "I wish I'd known you before."

A wisp of loss swept through her. "You know me now, and I'll be your pain-in-the-butt sister the rest of your life."

He gave a crooked grin. "Why do I feel like I suddenly won the genetic lottery?" Max asked.

"Because you did. In every way," Benjamin said and turned to his bride. "Just tell me you don't expect me to bow to you now."

"Only at certain moments," she said and laughed.

Benjamin took her mouth again, and Coco knew she had finally found home with the man of her heart and her dreams.

* * * * *

COMING NEXT MONTH from Harlequin® Special Edition®

AVAILABLE OCTOBER 16, 2012

#2221 THE PRINCE SHE HAD TO MARRY

The Bravo Royales

Christine Rimmer

The last person Princess Liliana would ever wed is her childhood nemesis. But now she is carrying his child. And the dark and brooding Bravo-Calabretti prince will do whatever he has to do to marry her and make things right.

#2222 A MAVERICK FOR THE HOLIDAYS

Montana Mavericks: Back in the Saddle

Leanne Banks

When injured veteran Forrest Traub encounters sweet Angie Anderson, she turns his plans to avoid romance upside down. But will Forrest's struggles with nightmares from his past come between him and Angie?

#2223 A GIFT FOR ALL SEASONS

Summer Sisters

Karen Templeton

The war had left single father Patrick Shaughnessy scarred, body and soul. He had wounds the sweet, bubbly April Ross could very well heal...but only if he accepted her selfless gift.

#2224 TEXAS CHRISTMAS

Celebrations, Inc.

Nancy Robards Thompson

When socialite Pepper Merriweather falls from grace after her father commits fraud, she discovers an ally in Robert Macintyre. Robert knows Pepper isn't responsible for her father's sins—and he knows from experience that everyone deserves a second chance.

#2225 A HOLIDAY TO REMEMBER

Helen R. Myers

Mack Graves had no intention of sticking around the east Texas ranch he'd recently inherited. But then he met Alana Anders. The enigmatic, retired marine had thought a wanderer's life would suit him better... until he kissed her.

#2226 MARRIAGE UNDER THE MISTLETOE

Helen Lacey

Gorgeous Californian firefighter Scott Jones is about ten years too young for Evie Dunn. But it seems Evie's long-dormant libido has other ideas!

When Forever, Texas's newest deputy, Gabe Rodriguez, rescues a woman from the scene of an accident, he encounters a mystery, as well.

Here's a sneak peek at A FOREVER CHRISTMAS by USA TODAY *bestselling author Marie Ferrarella, available November 2012 from Harlequin® American Romance®.*

It was still raining. Not nearly as bad as it had been earlier, but enough to put out what there still was of the fire. Mick was busy hooking up his tow truck to what was left of the woman's charred sedan and Alma was getting back into her Jeep. Neither one of them saw the woman in Gabe's truck suddenly sit up as he started the vehicle.

"No!"

The single word tore from her lips. There was terror in her eyes, and she gave every indication that she was going to jump out of the truck's cab—or at least try to. Surprised, Gabe quickly grabbed her by the arm with his free hand.

"I wouldn't recommend that," he told her.

The fear in her eyes remained. If anything, it grew even greater.

"Who are you?" the blonde cried breathlessly. She appeared completely disoriented.

"Gabriel Rodriguez. I'm the guy who pulled you out of your car and kept you from becoming a piece of charcoal."

Her expression didn't change. It was as if his words weren't even registering. Nonetheless, Gabe paused, giving her a minute as he waited for her response.

But the woman said nothing.

"Okay," he coaxed as he drove toward the town of Forever, "your turn."

The world, both inside the moving vehicle and outside of it, was spinning faster and faster, making it impossible for her to focus on anything. Moreover, she couldn't seem to pull her thoughts together. Couldn't get past the heavy hand of fear that was all but smothering her.

"My turn?" she echoed. What did that mean, her turn? Her turn to do what?

"Yes, your turn," he repeated. "I told you my name. Now you tell me yours."

Her name.

The two words echoed in her brain, encountering only emptiness. Suddenly very weary, she strained hard, searching, waiting for something to come to her.

But nothing did.

The silence stretched out. Finally, just before he repeated his question again, she said in a small voice, hardly above a whisper, "I can't."

Who is this mystery woman?
Find out in A FOREVER CHRISTMAS
by Marie Ferrarella, coming November 2012
from Harlequin® American Romance®.

HAREXP1112